SICK CRUSH

ALTA HENSLEY

To Mr. Alta Hensley. You were my sick crush for as long as I can remember. And I wouldn't have it any other way.

NEWSLETTER

ALTA HENSLEY'S HOT, DARK & DIRTY NEWS

Do you want to hear about all my upcoming releases? Get free books? Get gifts and swag from all my author friends as well as from me? If so, then sign up for my newsletter!

Alta's Newsletter

BLURB

IF I TOUCH HER... MY LIFE IS RUINED.

She's smart, beautiful, and just my type.

She's also barely legal.

The very definition of forbidden fruit.

And I don't just want a bite; I want to devour her.

Now she is standing before me, her gorgeous eyes filled with tears.

She's in trouble.

She has a stalker, a dangerous one, and he's getting closer.

She needs my help.

She's too innocent to know she should be more afraid of me.

I can no longer restrain myself.

I'm about to shatter my entire life, just because of a sick crush.

1

CORRINE

What makes a stalker tick?

How do they think?

What do they feel as they watch their prey?

Is it the same as how a hunter holds his breath right before he pulls the trigger? A momentary silence seconds before a deadly result.

Excitement mixed with fear.

Desire mixed with contempt.

The need to love and the need to hurt.

I wondered about these things as they were such a part of my life.

But I had no choice but to struggle to cope.

Every single door in the house was shut and locked. The curtains were pulled closed. The alarm system activated, but I still felt an evil trying to break in... watching... waiting... I could feel the demon there. It was so powerful. So consuming.

A normal person would call the police when they were afraid—when they worried a murder may occur. I knew I could call the police, and they'd walk the premises, and even would come inside and check the rooms for me. I knew this, because I'd called before.

Many times.

I'd warn them that a stalker was near.

And each time, the police would do their due diligence, pat me on the head, and be on their way. And each time, I felt that demon watching... laughing. The stalker wouldn't get caught. He was far too smart for that.

I had my own personal ghost.

A Boogie Man.

He only came out of the depths of the underworld for me.

I guess I should consider myself special.

Not every girl gets her very own beast to tango with.

My mother would call it star attention. Being a celebrity, she always told me that there was no such thing as bad attention, and you could spin anything in your favor. But that was the life she craved. Not me. I simply wanted to feel safe and to be left alone by fake people. Did I want love and attention from the *right* people? Of course I did. But not from the superficial and the plastic.

Peeking through the crack of thick curtains to see if I could see anything, I knew I needed to get the courage to go outside. I was late for school again, and I couldn't stay hidden away in the house all day. I'd already missed enough school, and since it was my senior year, I really didn't want to get held back again due to poor attendance. Being a nineteen-year-old senior was embarrassing enough. I had one last shot at this, or a GED was in my future.

Fast.

Everything needed to be fast in order to break away. I grabbed my backpack, car keys, and all but sprinted to my vehicle. Would my monster follow? Maybe, but I couldn't allow him to have all the control. Somehow, I had to gain some of the power back. Plus, I never felt like he was with me at my school—Black Mountain Academy—while I was there. If he was, I didn't feel his presence or see his shadow out of the corner of my eye like I did when at home.

I didn't need to look at the time to know school had already started for the day. The lack of students milling around their expensive cars or gossiping on the massive stairs leading up to the main building, told me all I needed to know. I would need to go to the office *again*, ask for a tardy slip *again*, and promise not to be late *again*.

"Miss   Parker..."   the   secretary—Mrs. Whatshername—said. "This is the third time this week you've been here."

"I know. Sorry," I mumbled as I approached the counter to sign in. "Do you want me to write another note excusing myself?" There were perks to being a legal adult. She had to accept my letter rather than needing it from my mother or guardian. I legally could write it myself.

She pursed her lips and shook her head. "One minute."

Walking away, she left me standing there awkwardly, anxious to at least be able to attend the last fifteen minutes of first period.

"Corrine Parker," a deep voice called, snapping me from my thoughts. I looked over at Mr. D—the principal—standing in the doorway to his office, motioning for me to enter. Mrs. Whatshername stood next to him with crossed arms and a smug smile on her face. "Please come to my office."

Releasing a sigh, and trying to not roll my eyes at how Mrs. Whatshername seemed to get joy in this, I obediently did as I was asked. This wouldn't be my first trip to the principal's office, but my first at this school. I knew it would be better for me and faster if I just smiled, apologized, swore I never would do it again, and allowed the lecture to come with no smart-ass or defensive remarks.

Although his office appeared like any other stuffy, sterile, and rich academy office I've seen before, Mr. D was far from the ordinary principal I was used to. For one, he was good-looking. And yes, I knew that students weren't supposed to look at teachers or administrators in that way, but Black Mountain Academy was full of beautiful people—

both students and faculty—and Mr. D was no different. Plus, the man appeared slightly rough around the edges. His dark hair was always slightly messy, his tie a bit loose, and his shirt never quite pressed to perfection. He almost seemed as uncomfortable with his required attire as the rest of the students felt in the uniforms we were forced to wear. And sitting near him now as he still stood on the side of the desk, I could see some colorful ink peeking out from beneath his rolled sleeves. I couldn't quite make out what it was on his forearm, but it was most definitely a tattoo or possibly even several.

He was a mystery.

A puzzle I wanted to solve.

I had to look up at him as he towered over me. His whiskey-hued eyes screamed disapproval as he crossed his arms. Hoping he would take his seat across from me, I shifted uncomfortably in my chair.

"How long have you been a student at Black Mountain Academy?" he asked, and I wasn't sure if he already knew the answer.

"Three months," I answered. I considered adding "sir", but figured he wasn't a man who required that level of stuffy protocol. He seemed much more casual.

"And out of those three months, how many days would you say you've been absent or tardy?"

"Too many," I said, pretty sure he didn't want an exact number but was merely wanting me to acknowledge it was not acceptable.

He remained quiet for an awkward amount of time and stood over me which caused my palms to get clammy and my mouth to go dry.

For the love of God sit down.

I hated when all eyes were on me. Even though I was nearly a twin of my mother, and everyone claimed I had the face and body for the big screen, I never wanted to follow in my mom's footsteps. Her agent even suggested he represent me so he could make my "darker, more exotic version of Marilyn Monroe beauty" work in my favor. He wasn't the first man in Hollywood who told me he could make me famous with "a face and body like that" as they also tried to make a move on a minor. It was sick but sadly part of my life. I grew up knowing I had sexual appeal, and watching my mother work a room had tutored me on how to get my way with men by using it.

Even knowing all that, I still hated when all eyes were on me.

But Mr. D studied my every move. I could feel the burn of his eyes even though I tried to avoid connecting mine with his. I didn't want to fake flirt to try to get out of this, but I wasn't opposed to it either if it meant I could walk out of this office free and clear of anything more than a stern lecture.

I was now on his radar, and that was okay, as long as there weren't any other negative ramifications.

"Why are you always late? And missing so much school?" he asked.

I couldn't tell him the truth. I had learned a long time ago about speaking of anything real about my life. Either people thought I had lost my mind, that I was on drugs, or that I was a compulsive liar looking for attention. No one believed me. They all thought every issue or feeling I had was all in my head.

And maybe it was.

"I've been sick lately," I answered. "Maybe I need vitamins."

Okay, so my answer sucked, but I didn't know what else to say.

"I'm assuming you want to graduate."

"Obviously, or I wouldn't be here," I said, hating that my words came out far snarkier than intended.

"Do you feel you're on the path to graduation?"

"Yes, I mean... that's the plan," I answered, not liking that he was hinting at me not being able to do so... *again*.

"We're going to have to call your parents," he said, finally walking over to his chair, sitting, and typing on his computer to no doubt pull up my file.

"I'm nineteen," I offered. "I don't have a guardian anymore."

I knew I risked pissing him off with the statement, which was not my intent. I wasn't challenging him, but just wanted to save him the time and effort of figuring it out for himself.

He stopped typing, stared directly into my eyes, leaned back into his leather high-back chair and said, "I understand that. But you're still a student here, and there are still rules that need to be followed. My guess is that, although you are an adult by legal definition, it's still your parents who pay for your tuition here. Am I correct?"

I nodded. "My mother does. My father isn't in the picture." Actually, I didn't even know who my father was. Nor did my mother as monogamy wasn't a word in her vocabulary. But I didn't need to go into that bit of detail with the man.

"Well, then I believe your mother should be made aware that you're about to be expelled from Black Mountain Academy if you miss any more school or are late again."

I swallowed the lump forming in the back of my throat. I hadn't realized I was so close to being kicked out.

"It won't happen again," I began. "I understand that—"

"An attendance contract will need to be signed by both you and your mother in order for you to remain at the school." He reached for the phone, lifted the receiver, and looked at me expectantly. "At what number can I reach your mother?"

Not being able to resist smirking, I leaned back in my chair and raised an eyebrow. "Good luck trying. I could give you her cell, and I could even give you her business line. Hell, I could give you her agent's number, her manager's, her assistant's... but you won't be able to reach her."

I had tried to be respectful, but now he was just pressing my buttons. I didn't like talking about my mother—or lack of a mother—and I was growing more annoyed by the second.

Hanging up the phone, he asked, "So, you live by yourself?"

I shrugged. "I'm nineteen, remember?"

I didn't reveal the fact that I pretty much had lived by myself for most of my life. Occasionally, I would be lucky enough to have a nanny or a housekeeper watch over me. But a mother? No.

"Did she move here with you to Black Mountain?"

"We didn't just move here. It's been a vacation home for years," I said, knowing I wasn't exactly answering the question.

"But you moved here to go to school. Not vacation. Correct?"

I nodded.

"Corrine…" He reached for his coffee cup and took a sip before continuing on. "Where's your mother?"

"I don't know. French Riviera. Greece maybe. On a yacht with some billionaire possibly." I shrugged. "Your guess is as good as mine."

"And she doesn't answer her phone?"

You would think a mother would, but no.

I took a calming breath and shook my head. "She likes to detach from the world between films. Her last movie took a lot out of her." Or so she told me when I last spoke to her before moving to Black Mountain.

I had told her I wanted a change and would like to attend a new school. She agreed, thought a change of scenery would do me good, but did nothing beyond that to help me... unless you counted the use of her credit card as help.

"And what if you need her?" he asked.

I gave up on needing her a long time ago. Of course, that was yet another little tidbit of information I didn't share with Mr. D.

"I'm fine."

Mr. D did a good job hiding his emotions. I knew he was judging me, but his face remained flat, hard, and it drove me crazy that I couldn't read him. Although I really didn't care what he thought about me just as long as he didn't kick me out of Black Mountain Academy.

"Regardless, I'm going to need to speak to your mother," he said.

"I understand that. But like I told you, it isn't going to be easy."

He took a deep breath, exhaled slowly and nodded. "I'm not sure I believe that you have zero way of contacting her. But regardless, until I speak with her, you have detention—every day until a conference is set up with your mother."

I opened my mouth to argue, but he put up a hand.

"Unless you want me to move forward with expulsion due to your lack of attendance."

I shut my mouth, looked down at my feet and ran my palms over my school uniform skirt. Taking hold of the fabric, I raised it up my thigh to reveal more flesh. I snuck a peek to Mr. D and waited to see how he'd react before pulling my skirt up a little further. Maybe it was time to bring in the big guns.

Except he didn't even look at me. He didn't seem to notice or care. Trying to flirt with what I figured to be more of a robot rather than a man, would just be embarrassing. Seeing as his eyes didn't even glance toward my legs, I doubted I would have much success.

Damn.

"Fine," I mumbled. Although the likelihood of me attending detention every day until graduation was more likely than him reaching my mom.

"Get to class," he said, rising from his chair. "And so we are on the same page"—he walked toward the door as I followed—"if you miss another day, or are late again, you'll not be allowed to attend this school any longer. Are we clear, Miss Parker?"

I walked past him in the doorway and bit my tongue against what I really wanted to say. "Yes, Mr. D. Perfectly clear."

2

Mr. D

It had been a huge mistake thinking I would like this job in Black Mountain better than my former position in Oakland. I had assumed getting out of the inner-city school for some posh academy gig would make life easier. The pay was stellar, the fresh mountain air was needed, and a change of scenery crucial if I was to have any more years left in me for academia life.

I was wrong.

It was still the same bullshit.

The same kids, the same excuses, the same teachers, the same paperwork that nearly sucked the life out of me, and the same crap that I loathed.

The only real difference in being the principal of Black Mountain Academy was that I dealt with rich little fucks rather than poor ones. But that wasn't really the worst part of the job. What I really hated was the damn board of directors and their pointless meetings and social gatherings. The board of Black Mountain Academy won the award as being the most precocious, elite, and annoying people I had ever met.

Yeah... I clearly needed a new profession or, at the very least, a new attitude. Nothing seemed to make me happy any longer. Even a move as big as the one I'd made in the beginning of the school year. I thought change would do me good, but so far, the only thing I'd gained was a constant headache and a new thirst for whiskey on the rocks.

Black Mountain Academy had hired me because they felt they needed someone who couldn't be pushed around by the parents of the student body. We weren't dealing with the average blue-collar mom and dad at this school. No. We had some of the most powerful people's kids attending, and the academy was known for blowing through their staff because they couldn't take the entitled bullshit for long. I, on the other hand, refused to be a casualty because I was shoved out. So, the board was wise in hiring me for that reason alone.

After Corrine Parker left my office, I had been busy the rest of the day with putting out constant fires. Finally, having a moment of time after school let out, I walked over to my computer and found the phone number on file and dialed. I didn't think Corrine would lie to me, but I'd be an idiot not to at least try. I'd become accustomed to neglectful parents while working in my school in Oakland. Foster kids, or kids in worse situations were a majority rather than a minority, and it was something I was used to working around. But I hadn't expected it in an upper-class school like Black Mountain.

I guess shitty parents existed everywhere.

When I heard the message that the voicemail box was full, I slammed the phone down in frustration. What kind of mother couldn't care less about her daughter? I felt sorry for Corrine, and second-guessed my decision about giving her detention until I reached her mom. It was likely I never would. And while my position as principal meant I was considered a mandatory reporter, Corrine was nineteen, so it wasn't like I could report her to the state to step in for neglect. Basically, this was a girl who no longer was part of the system.

Most likely not part of anything.

Another difference between this school and the one in Oakland was the fact that a Google search offered a plethora of information on the student body's families. These parents were famous for one thing or another. All were notorious whether it was by celebrity status, crime status, or empire building domination. So, deciding that maybe I could hunt down Corrine's mother by finding out where she was currently located, I turned to the internet to research her.

It didn't take long to see that Corrine wasn't lying. There were tons of articles about her mother traveling around the world with the leading actor from her last movie. They were supposedly in love and living it up on yachts and private jets. Pictures flooded my search of her mother drinking champagne, stumbling in and out of limos and topless in a thong bikini while sunbathing. She was the spitting image of Corrine with her long dark chestnut hair, mysterious brown eyes, and in almost all the pictures, her lips were parted in the same exact sexy smirk I'd seen Corrine wearing when sitting across the desk from me. Candy Parker was fucking stunning, but women like that knew it. Hence all the half-naked photos of her floating around the internet.

There were no mentions of Corrine in any of the articles, but frankly I didn't dig for long. It made me sick seeing this so-called mother's face so happy without her daughter by her side.

Having had enough for one day, I packed up my stuff and decided to leave before the sun set for a change. I was due for some booze and couch time. As glamorous as my life was not, it wasn't like there was a lot to do around Black Mountain anyway. Unless you counted all the dinner invitations and parties I was invited to by every member of the board of directors, the parents trying to get in good with me, or the bored trophy wives who wanted some male companionship, my social life sucked. I abhorred those parties. I despised the dinners. And I detested fake women flirting with me. This world was everything I wasn't, but unfortunately, I had to play the game and attend many events I hated. Tomorrow there was a board of directors' gathering at the Johnson estate, and I was dreading it. So, at least tonight I was going to take the evening for myself.

As I walked out to the parking lot, I noticed Corrine bending over her car with the hood up. School had been let out hours ago, but she'd also had detention. The only cars left in the parking lot were mine, Corrine's, and the janitor's. Even though the last thing I wanted to do was deal with car issues, I figured that part of the reason she was out here alone was due to me, so the least I could do was offer some help.

Trying not to look at how her bent over position had her ass nearly on full display beneath her short, pleated uniform skirt, I made my way over to her.

"Any idea what's wrong with your car?" I asked as I walked up behind her. The car didn't seem to fit her. Most of the students drove cars that were worth more than the teachers here made in a year, but Corrine's was a classic Mercedes. Old, but definitely classy.

She jumped and screamed, turning to face me with wide dark eyes.

I put out my hands in a gesture to show her I wasn't a threat. "Sorry. Didn't mean to scare you."

She took a deep breath and relaxed a bit when she saw it was just me, although I could see she still trembled slightly. "It's my mom's car. Or one of them. I think it sat too long in the garage up here. We haven't been to the house in years, and I think they were neglected. I actually had to brush off dust when I finally found the keys."

"Did you check the oil?" I asked, considering the obvious culprits. "Gas?"

She nodded. "Yes, I did that on day one, but I think all the plugs and stuff need to be changed. Or maybe it's the battery." She looked at me. "Can I get a jump?"

"Let me get my car," I said as I turned and walked over to my own vehicle.

The air was getting cool as the sun lowered over the horizon, and I really didn't want to be dealing with this, but it wasn't like I could just leave the girl stranded in the parking lot either. Especially knowing she didn't have any parents to call for help. I had to hand it to her. At least she tried to be somewhat self-reliant. She could have been sitting in her car helpless, crying, and calling Daddy for help.

"All right," I said, as I got out of my car, yanked out my jumper cables, and clipped them on the posts of her battery. "Go ahead and try to start it."

She tried multiple times, and nothing. I was far from being a mechanic, but I didn't think it was the battery. From the clicking sound, it seemed to be more the starter than anything, and if that was the case, we wouldn't be able to fix it in the parking lot.

"I think we need to call and get it towed," I said, knowing I was in for a much longer evening now that I would have to take her home after waiting for a tow truck to come.

"I have AAA," she said as she pulled out her phone and dug around in her glove box for the card. "Unless my mom let it lapse or something," she added under her breath.

I walked over to my car, turned it off, and leaned against my hood while she was on the phone. When she hung up, she looked up at me and smiled.

"Thank you. They should be on their way soon. You don't have to wait here."

"Someone needs to give you a ride," I said, crossing my arms across my chest and settling in for the wait.

"I can call someone," she said, but I could tell she was lying.

She was still the new girl in this school, and I was pretty sure I had only seen her interact with a couple of people. She wasn't exactly the loner type, but the school was brutal when it came to trying to fit in to any of the social circles. I'd seen no evidence that she had a best friend close enough who would be willing to drop everything and come help her.

"I'll wait and then take you home," I said.

As I had done, she closed her door of the car and braced against the hood. "Well, thank you. I appreciate it."

"So, do you have any other family who live in Black Mountain?" I asked, deciding now would be a good time to try to pump more information out of her in a non-threatening manner.

"No. The house we have up here is just one of many vacation homes. It was one of my favorites, though. I really like the area. It's pretty."

"So, did you come here by yourself?" I asked.

She looked at me skeptical at first, but then nodded. "I needed a change. My mom was on set when I decided to make the move. She was cool with it though."

"Where did you go to school before that?"

"L.A., but I've been to a lot of schools."

"What about friends and family in L.A.?" I asked.

"It's just me and my mom. No family, and friends come and go." She looked around as if she was praying the tow truck would arrive and save her from the interrogation. I supposed that since no huge truck appeared, she felt compelled to fill the silence. "I have one friend who lives here. We went to school together in L.A. too. Kevin Stevenson. He's like me. His mom and dad are in the movie business as well. So, he understands... well, we have a lot in common. He was the one who gave me the idea about finishing out the year in Black Mountain. He said he was, since his family has a house up here too, and I thought it was a good idea."

I was familiar with the name Kevin Stevenson but couldn't recall much about him. But considering there were hundreds of kids who attended Black Mountain Academy, it didn't say all that much that he didn't stand out in my mind. It most likely meant the kid kept to himself, kept his nose clean, and would do just fine until he graduated. I did find it crazy that these kids could just pick up and leave one house to live in another when they got bored and decided a change would be good.

"You really don't have to wait around," she said. "I can figure it out."

Leaving her wasn't an option, so I just kept up with the questions. "I looked at your transcripts, and you get great grades. Why did you get held back a year?"

"Life," she mumbled as she opened her passenger door and pulled out her backpack and a stack of books to take with her when the tow truck arrived.

I could tell she wasn't going to give me any more than that as an answer.

"What about you?" she asked, clearly changing the subject. "Do you like Black Mountain?"

I gave a slight nod. "I do. It's different than Oakland which is where I'm from. But I do like it here for the most part." I didn't know why I was lying, but I couldn't exactly tell her that I thought the area sucked. The last thing I needed was for that bit of gossip to be spread throughout the school.

Mr. D thinks Black Mountain sucks ass.

She chuckled as she reached behind her head and pulled her dark brown hair up into a ponytail. "*For the most part.*" She was clearly clever enough to pick up on my hidden dig.

I had studied how to read students for years, and knew she was trying to hide her nervous energy by talking and fiddling with her hair. I was getting too close by asking the questions, and it was obvious that, though Corrine was adept in hiding her feelings, she was slowly revealing just how uncomfortable I made her.

The rumble of a truck in the distance made her perk up as she looked toward the approaching sound. "That was fast," she said. "We would have been here all night if this was L.A."

The same could be said for Oakland, and I was glad that I would be home soon instead of wasting away my entire evening.

Once the truck was loaded with her car and leaving the parking lot, I opened the passenger door for Corrine. "Ready?"

She nodded and climbed into my car with her books and bag in hand. "Thank you. I appreciate it."

She didn't live too far from the school, but as she rattled off directions, I knew it was too far for her to walk. "Do you have another car available to drive to school tomorrow?"

"I should. There are several in the garage. I'm sure one of them will run and the battery won't be dead. If not, I can call Kevin in the morning. I'm sure he'll give me a lift."

It bothered me that I was talking to a student who was completely on her own. I also didn't like that she had no one to turn to other than a casual friend. It made me sad for her. As someone who kept to himself and didn't have a large family or friend pool either, I understood how lonely it could be when you needed someone in your corner.

"Okay, well, I'm going to give you my number in case you need any help," I said, attempting to not think about the ramifications of giving a student my number. "Try not to plaster it throughout the school, okay?" Inwardly, I cringed at the thought of seeing my number written all over the bathroom stalls to "call for a good time".

"I'll keep it private," she reassured me. "But I also won't bother you. I'll be fine. I've dealt with much worse than a broken-down car in my life. This is a piece of cake."

Those words also bothered me. No young lady should feel that way. She should feel stressed, worried, hell… I wouldn't blame her if she cried. Car stress could be one of the worst stresses. Granted, she didn't have to worry about money or how she would come up with the funds to fix it, so at least she had that going for her.

As we pulled up to her house… actually, mansion would be a better word to describe the massive structure in front of me, I tried not to picture Corrine all alone living inside of it. This was just a vacation home, and my entire condo could fit in one room of it. I wasn't shocked, however. It was classic Black Mountain lodging for our student body. The house was also gated, so I pulled up to the key box and looked at her for the code.

"5555," she said.

I punched it in, and then said, "You may want to come up with something a little less easy."

"Yeah, well, my mom has an awful memory, so welcome to the access I just gave you to break into all aspects of our life." She chuckled as the gates opened and I drove up the circular driveway.

"Have a good night," I said as she hopped out of the car and turned to face me.

"I will. Thank you, Mr. D. You didn't have to stay, but I'm glad you did."

I gave a slight nod and watched her walk up to the door. I waited to make sure she got inside safely and really hated the fact that she was entering a very large and empty house. At least I was going home to a cozy place where my voice wouldn't echo in the hallways. I felt sorry for Corrine, although I wasn't sure how I could help in this situation. Unlike some of the students I had dealt with in Oakland, at least Corrine had a roof over her head and money to buy food. She didn't need to be my charity case even though something in my gut told me to keep an eye on her.

3

CORRINE

It was fair to say that today was a pretty shitty day. Nearly getting kicked out of school, detention, broken down car, and now I looked into an empty refrigerator hating the fact that I was going to have to order a pizza again. There were only so many topping combinations one could do to try to mix up the repetitive meal. Pizza was pizza, and I was sick of it.

Picking up my phone, I decided it was best to call my mom's manager first. Bill was a twerp who was way too handsy with me when I was around him, but he was also the only way of reaching my mother when she was out and about and off the radar. I had free rein with her credit card, so paying for the car to get fixed wasn't an issue, but I thought it best to at least let her know. Or to let Bill know.

Most likely I was wasting my time.

Which is why I was happy when I got Bill's voicemail, because the rare times I had to actually speak with him, I always got a sick feeling in my stomach. I truly felt that he imagined me naked when I spoke. He was a creep but one of the best managers in the biz, or so my mother always told me. I still always pictured him in some dark basement somewhere jacking off to kiddie porn.

When I got done leaving him a message about the car, the school needing to talk with my mother, and hung up, my phone rang right away. I considered not answering it if it was Bill calling me right back, but I saw it was Kevin.

"Hey," I said, sitting at the expansive kitchen counter and running my fingertips over the smooth white marble.

"Where were you after school?" he asked. "I was looking for you. A few of us were getting together, and I wanted to see if you wanted to come."

"I got detention."

"Detention? Why?"

"For being late and missing so much school. And then my car broke down... and let's just say it's been a crappy day."

"That sucks. Why didn't you call me? I would have come and picked you up."

It was odd hearing Kevin act as if the logical thought process would be to call him up and lean on him for help. For some reason, I didn't think we were *that* close, but it was most likely all in my head and feeling like no one was really in my life whom I could count on. We were friends, actually pretty close friends in many ways, but then like strangers as well. I'd nearly had a total breakdown when rumors began circulating about me and my name got decimated at our previous school, and when Kevin suggested we move to Black Mountain, I had jumped all over his plan. He needed a change, and so did I. But at the same time, we both just did the move on our own. We kept our distance during it all.

Our relationship was definitely complicated.

We were friends... but not daily friends. We could go a number of days never speaking, but then if I had to be honest, he was the only real friend I had. He was trying very hard to make friends in Black Mountain, and I wasn't. He had invited me several times to hang out with people, but I always felt like I would be a tagalong. I tried... I just wasn't very good at the social game. Kevin wasn't very good either, to be honest, but at least he was giving it his all this time at Black Mountain.

"I considered it, but I got a ride home. Thanks though."

There was a long pause, and then Kevin said, "Okay then... well... do you need a ride or something tomorrow? I can swing by and get you before school."

"I think I'll be fine. I have other cars to choose from. But I'll let you know if none of them start or something."

"Do you want to hang out tomorrow after school?" he asked. "I've met a couple of cool people I could introduce you to."

I sighed. "I have detention."

"For how long?"

"I don't know. Mr. D says he has to reach my mother to talk about my attendance before detention stops."

"Shit," Kevin breathed out. "That could be the rest of the year. Did you explain how your mom just checks out?"

"Sort of. But I don't think he gets it."

"Yeah, most don't. Couldn't tell you where my parents are at the moment." He paused for an awkward moment of silence. "Sorry. Is there anything I can do?"

"I'm good. Thanks for checking in on me. I appreciate it."

"No prob. I'll talk to you later. I hope he gets hold of your mom soon."

Hanging up with Kevin left me alone.

In an empty and silent house.

Story of my life.

Really not wanting pizza, I walked over to the pantry in hopes of finding something hidden in the far corners of the shelves.

The pantry door was open.

I froze, my heart stopped, and a scream strangled with my lack of breath.

I never left *any* door open. Not one. All doors in all the house remained closed at all times. It was my obsessive rule.

All doors must be closed!

I ran to the hallway and noticed that every single door to every single bedroom was open.

Open!

Oh God, why were they not closed?

I sprinted up the stairs to discover that every door was open as well.

The alarm system? Jesus, I got sloppy when Mr. D dropped me off. I didn't set it. I walked into the house and didn't immediately lock the door and set it. For the first time, in a long time, someone did something kind for me. Someone was putting me first, and it—

I let down my guard.

I nearly fell running back down the stairs, but I had to get out of the house. I could feel the walls closing in. The darkness was here. I could feel it.

Eyes were on me. They were on me. They were *still* on me.

But as I neared the bottom of the stairs, I saw the shadow of a man approaching the house through the small window by the door.

Nearly flying, I bolted the door lock. "I called the police!" I screamed. "They're on their way, so get the fuck out of here!"

I held my breath and waited.

Please leave. Please leave. Please leave.

A pounding on the door had me screaming. "I have a gun!" I lied. "I'll shoot!"

"Corrine? Open up. It's Mr. D. What's going on in there? Open up!"

Tears of relief streamed down my face as I unlocked the door with shaky hands. My knees threatened to buckle, my ears rang, but at least there was someone outside who could help me.

When I opened the door, Mr. D charged inside, scanning the room with fisted hands and raging eyes.

"Who's here?" he demanded.

"No one," I barely managed to squeak as the tears kept flowing. I struggled to regain regular breathing so I wouldn't hyperventilate and collapse in my foyer. I wasn't sure if I could tell him the truth. The truth got me nowhere in life.

He spun on his heels and took hold of my upper arms, forcing me to look him directly in the eyes. "Who were you screaming at? Why did you call the police?" He looked down at my hands. "Where's the gun?"

I couldn't imagine the thoughts that had to be running through Mr. D's mind. From the look of him, and the way his eyes were wide, his jaw locked, and his entire body tense, I had scared him. And if I looked anything like how I felt... well, I had to appear a hot mess.

"There isn't a gun. I got worked up on... something... I thought you were..." I paused as I still struggled to breathe.

He released the tight hold of my arms and placed his palm reassuringly on my back as his stance and facial expression softened.

"I thought you were someone... I was yelling at you by mistake."

"Who did you think I was?" He waited and when I didn't immediately answer, he continued. "Who did you think I was that had you so terrified you called the cops?"

I shook my head. "I didn't call the cops. I was saying that to scare you, and I was just..." Fuck, I didn't even know how to explain this nightmare.

I glanced at another open door off the living room, and my world began to spin.

"Who are you so afraid of?" Mr. D prodded again.

I took a step away from him feeling as if his very presence was the reason I couldn't quite get my breath. "I just got spooked. I thought someone was in the house, and then I saw your shadow, and... my imagination got the best of me."

I needed to tell Mr. D something... anything other than I may be losing my mind.

"You thought someone was in your house?" He was already scanning the immediate area with his piercing eyes. "Can I look around?"

I nodded with maybe too much zeal.

God yes. Please look around. Please don't leave me alone. I can't be alone.

"Did you hear noises?" he asked as he walked the front hallway with me following close behind.

I didn't want to be left alone for even a second, not even as he checked out the house.

"No. I noticed that all the doors were open in the house." I instantly regretted answering him the minute the words left my mouth.

He turned and looked at me with an eyebrow raised and narrowed eyes. "Do you normally keep them all closed or something?"

I took a deep breath and nodded. "It's a big house. It makes me feel safer."

Seemingly satisfied with my answer, Mr. D continued walking in and out of every room, careful to open every closet and look under and behind every big piece of furniture. I stayed glued to his side, even though with every room searched and deemed safe, I was able to feel my heart beginning to beat normally again, and the shaking of my body stopped. Mr. D seemed to care, and that act alone seemed to make everything raging inside of me ease.

"Do you have an alarm system?" he asked as he made his way upstairs.

"I do, but I forgot to set it after you dropped me off."

"What about video cameras?"

"I want them. But since this is just a vacation home we rarely used, my mom never got around to installing them. I tried to set them up myself, but..." I shook my head. "No, I don't have cameras yet."

Answering the question out loud made me realize how stupid I was. Why in the hell would I not install cameras? I was a young woman living alone, and I only relied on an alarm system that most likely was outdated.

"So, you close every door in the entire house?" he asked.

"Yes. I know I closed them all this morning."

"But you were running late for school this morning. Could you have forgotten?" he asked, not knowing just how obsessive compulsive I was over the closing of doors and *that* was one of the main reasons I was always late for school. I had to check and double check so many times, I wouldn't even be able to keep count.

"I'm positive," I answered simply.

"Do you have a cleaning lady?" he asked as we made our way into my bedroom.

I pointed to the pieces of clothing thrown haphazardly around. "Obviously not."

He gave a slanted grin but continued on with his investigation.

"Why did you come here?" I asked, suddenly realizing I didn't even know why he came back after dropping me off.

"You forgot your chemistry book in my car. I figured you may need it for homework tonight. Since I had the gate code, I just drove in. Then I heard you screaming and well... I readied myself for a fight."

We made our way to the kitchen, and at this point I was feeling much better, but my body nearly itched with the need to run and close every door again. I didn't want to do it in front of Mr. D for fear of him not only wanting to speak to my mother about attendance but also about committing me.

He looked around the large room and seemed amused. "This is a huge kitchen for what I can only assume is very little cooking. Unless you're some secret chef I didn't know about."

I appreciated his ability to try to lighten the mood and offered a smile that I figured he was on the hunt for.

His face grew serious as he studied me. "Everything looks fine here, but are you okay?"

I nodded as I folded my arms over my chest, suddenly feeling cold. "I'll be fine. Like I said... just my imagination I guess."

He seemed to study me for a long moment before releasing a deep breath. "Is there anyone you can call? Maybe go spend the night someplace? You still seem shaken."

"I'll be fine. I'm used to being here alone."

He was analyzing me... I could tell. I'd been *analyzed* by enough people in my lifetime to know.

He walked to the counter and sat on a barstool. "Well, the least you can do is offer me a drink for saving your life." He smiled, and I had to admit it warmed the chill that was taking over my body.

"I uh..." I opened the refrigerator even though I knew nothing was in it. "I don't really have anything to offer." I turned to face him. "I guess I could go down to the cellar and get a bottle of wine." The thought of going downstairs in that dank and cold room alone terrified me, but it was the least I could do.

He stared into the empty fridge that I still held open. "What do you eat?"

I shrugged like it was no big deal that I stood in a mansion, but my refrigerator was completely bare. "Pizza. Or Chinese food."

In reality, I hated the Chinese restaurant that delivered, but I had to make it sound like I didn't just live off of pizza alone. Thank goodness for the lunch at school or I would most likely die of vitamin deficiency.

We stared at each other in silence for what felt like an eternity until I couldn't take it any longer.

"Where's my chemistry book?"

His narrowed eyes that hadn't broken their stare on me widened. "Oh, I must have dropped it by the door when I charged in."

Grateful to have a reason to leave the kitchen, I walked to the door, which was still wide open, and saw my book cast aside on the porch.

When I bent over to pick it up, I heard the words, "Why don't you come out to dinner with me? I know of this great restaurant about twenty minutes outside of Black Mountain. A small drive, but worth it. They have a steak and baked potato that can't be mimicked."

Ahhh, the pity invite.

"I've taken up enough of your evening, Mr. —"

"We'll be far enough from Black Mountain that you don't have to worry about anyone seeing you eat dinner with your principal and then teasing you tomorrow."

I huffed. "I seriously doubt anyone would pay enough attention to me to even notice what I do or don't do. But—"

"I'm starving. I'm sure you are too," he interrupted. "Come on. My treat."

I walked past him in the doorway and put the book on a nearby table. I looked at the open doors I could see, knowing there were more, and the thought of being left alone in the house again made me feel sick to my stomach.

"Corrine. Come on. Grab a jacket and your purse or whatever. I'm not taking no for an answer. I need the company and a good meal. And after the evening you've had, you do too."

I glanced over my shoulder at him and knew he meant business. And at this point, I didn't want to resist.

He walked into the living room. "Let's shut all the doors and lock up before we go."

Bless the man. I wanted to do that so badly but didn't want to seem insane. I knew he was throwing me a bone, but I'd take it.

I quickly ran upstairs, with Mr. D doing the downstairs, and slammed all the doors shut with no intent of opening most of them again. My ears rang, my hands shook, and I worried madness would set in if I didn't leave the house with this man waiting. And as I closed the last door, I finally felt like I could breathe. I was safe for now. Even if I had demons lurking... they'd have to watch me walk away with Mr. D.

4

Mr. D

"You ate more than me." I laughed as I turned the car onto the highway leading us back to Black Mountain. "I didn't realize so much food could fit in a tiny body like yours."

"I couldn't help it. It was the best dinner I think I've ever had in my entire life," Corrine said as she stared out the passenger window with a smile on her face, and a casual demeanor about her. It had taken her almost half the meal before she seemed to relax around me, but it was nice to see she finally had.

"I told you it was good," I said. "But it needs to be kept our secret. I don't want it to become the next hot spot, and then we'll be forced to make reservations days in advance. I also don't want to see all those Black Mountain assholes—" I swallowed the rest of my sentence, realizing I didn't need to be revealing my true feelings on anything or anyone. "I think it's best to keep this little gem to ourselves."

"You don't have to worry about me," she said, her smile fading. "I don't really talk to anyone."

"Why is that?"

"I don't know. I guess, I just never fit in with the Hollywood life I was born into. You think Black Mountain Academy is full of spoiled brats, you should have seen some of the other schools I went to in L.A. and New York. London was the worst of them."

She let out a deep breath which had me stealing a glance at her. The streetlights lit up her face and the soft waves of her brown hair, which only seemed to expose the sadness inside her even more. The expression in her heavily-lashed eyes seemed so far off, yet present at the same time. I wanted to read this girl but struggled to.

She continued, "You wouldn't blame me for not wanting to really have any of them as my friends. And as for Black Mountain Academy... I'm new. It's hard to break into social circles that have been formed already. I'm older than them in more ways than one, and..."

I got the feeling she didn't care to try, but I wasn't going to push her on that anymore. I had gotten the feeling over dinner, that though Corrine was very easy to converse with, and it actually was a very pleasant night of casual conversation, the talk needed to remain light and only on the surface. She wasn't comfortable talking about her mother, her past, or her current situation. She was highly educated, very well-traveled, and frankly, far more cultured than me. Because of her mother, Corrine had traveled to most of the world, and yet, she didn't seem too excited to discuss her memories of those trips. She had also met some amazing people ranging from celebrities, chefs, artists, musicians, critically acclaimed authors, and political figures. Though she seemed to be a loner currently, the young woman had lived a lifetime already with her experiences and social interactions.

I truly found her fascinating and could have chatted with her all night had our meal not ended. When we reached her house, I was actually disappointed to have the evening end. It had been so easy, effortless, and genuine. As of late, all of my social engagements had been anything but.

"Thank you for the dinner," she said as I entered the gate code. It was also obvious that this girl had been trained on proper etiquette, had impeccable manners, and had the grace of a queen.

"Thank you for joining me."

"I'm sure it was the last thing you really wanted to do. Having dinner with a student was most likely not how you planned your night. But I appreciate it."

"Don't sell yourself short," I said, driving a little slower than need be just to be able to give the compliment. "You have a lot to offer, Corrine. I've met very few people like you."

"Like *me*?"

"True. Real. You aren't pretentious even though you know about a lot and have lived more life than most your age. You aren't immature, materialistic, or frankly... annoying. Listening to you this evening was actually a joy. I like you, Corrine Parker." I smirked and gave a small chuckle. "And I don't like most."

The car came to a stop, and Corrine ran her hands on top of her pleated uniform skirt that she'd not changed out of before leaving for dinner. I wished we had thought of that when we first entered the restaurant—as did she—but we both soon forgot about her attire, and it ended up being a non-issue.

"Thank you, Mr. D. Not too many people make me feel comfortable. But you did. I needed that."

I got out of the car and walked around to open the door for her. "If you don't mind, I'd like to do one more walk through of your house before I leave."

Shoulders that had tensed when we arrived at the house, visibly relaxed with my words. "I would like that. Thank you."

I bit my tongue on lecturing her about the fact that no motion lights came on as we approached the door. I had to remind myself that while she might live in this house, it wasn't her own. This responsibility fell directly on her mother. But considering Corrine was a young woman living alone, the very least she could have is proper lighting.

When she opened the door, I entered first and instantly noticed all the lights were out. I couldn't remember if we had left them on or not since the sun hadn't completely set yet when we left for dinner. But once Corrine flipped on the lights, I instantly saw something was wrong.

So wrong that the hairs on the back of my neck stood at attention.

The doors of the rooms were open.

Every. Single. Door.

"We closed every door," Corrine breathed out, clearly seeing what I did. "I know for a fact we did."

I looked up the stairs from the foyer and then into the hallway, and I saw doors open that I had personally closed.

"Go back to the car now," I ordered as I reached for my cell phone. "I'm calling the police."

She reached for my arm. "Please don't call the police."

"Corrine. Car. Now."

She snatched the phone from my grip and took a few steps back. "Let's leave, but don't call the cops."

"Someone's been in your house, or could still be. Of course I'm calling the police." I reached for the phone annoyed and also listening for the slightest movement in the eerie silence. "Give me my phone."

She glanced around the house with wide eyes and trembling lips. Without warning—and not giving me my phone—she ran out the door toward my car. I knew I needed to get her out of the house, and there was no way I was letting her back in until we got to the bottom of what was going on. I reached for the stack of books on the table, grabbed her school bag and followed her to the car.

Walking up to the passenger side of the car, I handed her things to her and then extended my hand. "I need to call the police. Someone could still be inside."

She shook her head. "You don't understand. I've called the police a lot in the past, and nothing good comes of it. My stalker isn't dumb enough to wait around for them. And all it does is risk one cop getting wind of who I am... or who my mother is, and the paparazzi will be all over this." She looked up at me. "You don't want media swarming around me, which then means around Black Mountain Academy, any more than I do."

She was right about that. I was paid a lot of money to make sure the students were shielded as much as possible from the limelight or any scandal of any sort. I most certainly couldn't be the one responsible for bringing the rag hags to our doorstep. There was an important Board of Directors meeting tomorrow, and the last thing I needed was a media circus outside the doors of the school during it.

"What do you mean by *stalker*?" I asked.

She swallowed hard and looked down at her hands which were clutching the strap of her bag.

"Is this something that has been happening multiple times?" I added.

"I've been a victim of many sick people in my past," she said softly. "Comes with who I am, I guess. But yes, ever since I arrived at Black Mountain, I've felt like someone's been watching me. He comes to me every day. I almost feel haunted." She paused and studied my face before continuing on. "You might think I'm crazy, or that I'm lying, but I swear to you, I'm not."

"And this person comes *into* your house? Have you seen him? Has he touched you? Harmed you?" Rage bubbled inside as I fisted my hands to try to control my tone of voice. Who the hell would torment a poor girl like this?

"I've never seen him. I've seen his shadows. I've heard him outside. But no, I don't think he's ever been inside the house until today. I'm usually really good at securing the alarm and making sure all the windows and doors are locked."

"How do you know it's a *he*?"

"I don't. It could be anyone," I admit. "I just call the demon lurking—he."

"This is why we need to call the police. If there's some crazy man stalking you, then they need to know about it." I reached out my hand again for the phone.

"They know. Trust me, they know," she said, her voice rising in frustration. "I've had them out to the house more times than I can count. By the time they get here, there's no sign of anything. Some of the police are sympathetic, and others get angry and accuse me of calling them for attention. The last cop actually said he would call the news next time I called since I clearly wanted all eyes on me." She shook her head and crossed her arms over her chest. "Even with you here, there's no good that will come from the cops coming." She looked back up at me. "Please, Mr. D. I'm scared, tired, and I don't want to deal with police and reports and... please."

"I can't just let you go back in there," I said, pointing at the house as if I were accusing it of a filthy crime. "There's no way I'm going to feel comfortable leaving you here even if I go in there and check every single inch of that house multiple times. He could come back after I'm gone."

"There's a bed and breakfast up the street I've stayed at before when I've gotten too scared to be alone. Would you mind taking me there?"

"And what if this stalker follows you there? What if he knows you go to that place for refuge? Corrine, this isn't safe!"

She flinched at my tone, and I took a deep breath to level out my emotions.

I hadn't meant to raise my voice, but the situation was becoming too much. I knew I should call the police. I knew I should do something, but at the same time, I knew how little the police could truly do if there was no real evidence of anything other than some open doors.

And it wasn't like we could get ahold of her goddamn mother!

I glanced back at the house and then at Corrine who suddenly seemed very small and vulnerable in my car. She was putting me in a very difficult situation. I couldn't just leave her here. I should call the authorities and at least report this. But I also knew that the people in Black Mountain were different than those in Oakland. I had to handle this differently.

"You're coming home with me to stay tonight. Tomorrow, we figure out how to reach your mother, and how to deal with this fucker who's messing with you."

I didn't really expect for her to argue, but I didn't expect for her to eagerly nod in agreement. "Okay, thank you."

The poor girl didn't want to be alone. I didn't blame her one bit, but I hated all who had put her in this position. I was damn near a stranger, and yet the only person she had to turn to in a time like this. For her to be this alone, this abandoned, and this terrified... I needed to make it right.

5

Burden was my middle name.

At least it was when it came to my mother. I knew it. My nannies knew it. Everyone in my life knew it.

But I had tried so hard—once I was of age—to never be a burden on anyone else again.

So, sitting in my principal's car, driving to his house, and frankly needing him so that I could make it through the night without having a complete breakdown, slammed me right back into burden category.

But at the same time, I had two options. I could be a burden, or I could be alone. For now, I'd choose burden.

Mr. D kept tapping his fingertips on the steering wheel, and his jaw was locked as he drove in silence. I knew what he was thinking. I couldn't blame him one bit, and frankly, he should stop the car and demand for me to get out.

"I don't want to get you in trouble," I said.

He quickly glanced my way and then back at the road. "We're not doing anything wrong."

"I'm not sure others would agree."

"Take the principal and student part out of this. You're a woman who's in danger, and I can't just let you risk your life by staying in that house. I'm helping you. Nothing wrong with that."

Was he saying it to me, or to himself?

"You're taking a student home with you. As innocent as this is, I understand the optics. I don't plan on telling anyone," I offered.

He nodded slowly. "I think it's best for both of us if we keep this to ourselves, yes." He looked over his shoulder as he took a sharp turn down a side street

I hadn't ever seen. It was quiet, no real traffic, and secluded. Perfect considering our current situation.

"No one has ever believed me about the stalker before," I confessed.

"Well someone opened those doors again. Both of us can't be losing our minds. I do wish you would have let me call the police, however. I'm starting to think there is no real way around that."

"Have you ever been surrounded by paparazzi, Mr. D?"

"No."

"Well, I have. And frankly, given a choice between one stalker and a bunch of stalkers with cameras, I choose the one I have."

"I get it. And it's the only reason I'm acting against my better judgment. I knew before accepting this position in Black Mountain that things would have to operate differently than I was used to. But we still have to figure something out."

"Maybe if I can get hold of my mom, I can get some security, or a bodyguard," I suggested, liking the idea even more as I said it out loud. I wouldn't be alone all the time.

"Yes, well, that goes back to us somehow getting in touch with her." He looked at me with accusing eyes. "Unless you weren't quite being honest on your ability of being able to reach her."

Wishing that was indeed the truth, I shook my head. "She'll come out of her cave soon. It won't be forever. I did leave a message with her agent. So, maybe he can reach her. I'm sure she's shopping movie deals right now and in some form of contact with him."

We pulled onto a street with well-manicured mini yards and rows of condominiums and townhouses. Everything was so orderly and uniform that it reminded me of a movie set. Though this area did not possess large mansions or expensive lodge-like houses, you could see that there was still a level of class and money present. It wasn't easy or cheap to live in Black Mountain, but I guess you could call this neighborhood the least expensive area.

"I have a two-bedroom condo," Mr. D said as he pulled into a single driveway and waited for the garage door to open. "It works for me. Simple, I don't have to worry about yard work, and it's clean."

I looked up at the light gray two-story condo that was lined up with others exactly the same but with a slightly different color. Though the condo was two stories, it appeared that it was actually one story of living space that sat on top of the garage.

I wasn't surprised when I got out of the car that Mr. D's garage appeared as organized and orderly as it was. Everything seemed to have a home. He had a mountain bike hanging on a rack on the side, and above my head hung two kayaks. There was also a punching bag in the far corner with some hand weights below it. It made sense that Mr. D would be so active considering he was obviously in such good shape. And it also made sense he would be into the outdoors since—other than myself—it seemed everyone in Black Mountain loved nature and outdoor living to some degree.

The garage door closed behind us as we walked up the stairs to the main level. Even though there were no fancy gates surrounding the house, or a keypad to get in, I hadn't felt this level of safe in a long time. Mr. D didn't seem like the violent type, but he also gave me the impression he wouldn't back down in a fight either.

As we walked into the condo, it was exactly as I pictured.

Masculine.

There was a brown leather couch that sat in front of a large-screen television. Next to the couch was a matching reclining chair, and by the wear and tear of the leather, I could see he enjoyed spending time in it. The living room also had a gas fireplace, cathedral ceilings making the room look much larger than it was, and an old chest being used as a coffee table. Mr. D took my books from me and set them on the table, and I dropped my bag beside them before continuing to look around. There was also a sliding glass door that led out to a deck or porch or something, but I couldn't tell because all I saw was pitch black on the other side of the glass.

I fought the urge to walk over to the large slider and pull the curtain shut. I never left windows open. Never.

But this wasn't my house, and we were on the second story, so even if someone wanted to peek in...

But there could be a tree out there, or another building, or...

"It's safe here. There are cameras all around the property, and a paid security guard patrols the area every hour on the hour. Plus, there is no way anyone can be a peeping Tom." Mr. D motioned for me to follow him out on the porch.

When we stepped out onto the small balcony with two chairs, a small table, and a BBQ, and even a bird feeder hanging, I could see what he meant by saying no one could see us. The balcony looked over a manmade pond that had a fountain in the center. There were no trees to climb blocking the view, and no other buildings to use as a hideout. I could stand outside like this and never be seen by anyone at all.

I could be outside... something I hadn't done since...

Mr. D walked back into the condo, and I followed. "So, I have two bedrooms, but I use the second room as my office. I don't have a bed in there."

"I'll sleep on the couch," I offered as quickly as I could. Middle name Burden that I was.

Adjacent to the living room was a small kitchen. It was clean, modern, and manly. Black granite countertops, stainless steel appliances, and not even a hand towel or any clutter at all. But there was one thing out of place.

I looked up at the ceiling and saw pasta noodles stuck all over.

I giggled. "Why is there spaghetti on the ceiling?"

He looked up, smiled, and said, "If you toss up the noodle and it sticks, then the pasta is done. It's how I cook."

I laughed again. I was far from a cook, but his method seemed... very bachelor-like.

"I don't keep much in the fridge, but compared to yours, I'm a supermarket in comparison. Help yourself to anything." He opened the fridge, pulled out a beer, and then looked at me. "Can I get you anything?" He even raised his beer. "Want one?"

I laughed, surprised that my principal was offering me alcohol. "No I.D. required?" I teased.

He shrugged. "If you're old enough to die for your country, then you're definitely old enough to have a damn beer. Plus, weren't you just telling me over dinner that you've tasted wine in world-renowned wineries that you have to practically give a body part to be invited to?"

I laughed but then shook my head. "Thanks, but no. I'm still stuffed from dinner."

Opening his beer, he led me down a short hallway. He pointed to the bathroom. "I only have one bathroom." He pointed again. "My room." His finger shifted toward another door. My office." He then gestured to closet doors that lined the hallway. "I have a washer and dryer behind there." He turned and glanced at what I was wearing. "We didn't think of packing a bag of clothes for you."

I looked down at my school uniform. "At least I have on what I need for tomorrow."

"I can give you a shirt of mine to sleep in, and if you want to wash your clothes so they'll be clean for tomorrow, you'll find everything you need above the washer."

Once again feeling like a burden, I didn't have much of a choice but to nod in agreement. "If you don't mind..."

He walked into his room, and I remained where I stood. It didn't seem appropriate following him into his private space. When he walked out, he handed me a gray Oakland Raiders t-shirt. I took it, feeling my face heat, and walked to the bathroom, silently laughing at the absurdity of the situation I was in.

Here I was, with Mr. D, my principal, on a school night, having a slumber party, wearing his shirt.

6

CORRINE

I wanted to take him up on that beer but wasn't sure how to ask now that the moment had passed. I sat on the couch, in his shirt and nothing else. I didn't have clean panties, so I had no choice but to wash those along with my school uniform. He wouldn't know that I was full commando, of course, but I did. And after the day I had, the evening I had, and now facing the night I had a fear I would have... I didn't think an entire six pack of beer could settle me down.

"I'm going into my office for a bit. I need to get a couple of things ready for a big meeting I have tomorrow," he said as he stood near the hallway leading to the bedrooms and bathroom.

I looked over my shoulder at him and nodded.

"Don't you have any homework to do?" he asked.

I couldn't help but roll my eyes. Really?

"Yes, Mr. D," I said in a sarcastic tone. "Whatever you say, sir." I couldn't help but laugh as I teased. I was sitting in the man's living room, wearing his clothes, and he was going to now act like a father figure.

He gave a small smile back. "I didn't mean it like that. I just... I mean..." He pointed to the backpack with the tip of his beer bottle, and in a very authoritative voice I had yet to hear from the man, he ordered, "Do your homework, Miss Parker, or else."

I laughed as he turned to make his way to the office. But he did have a point. I had a sizable amount of homework, and the thought of regaining some sense of normalcy to end a very frustrating, bizarre day, was very needed and even welcomed.

It was obvious that Mr. D didn't host dinner parties. The condo didn't have a dining room.

There was a small alcove off the kitchen with a round table and four chairs. Plenty of room for a single man, and the table seemed like a perfect spot to make my temporary desk. The alcove was surrounded by windows, however, and I wasn't sure about sitting in the middle of them front and center. Mr. D had made me feel comfortable about the sliding glass door in the living room being safe, but he hadn't done so about the rest of the windows.

Just as I was about to go interrupt him from his work and ask, the doorbell rang.

I froze with backpack in hand, not knowing what to do. I shouldn't be there. I was wearing the man's t-shirt. There was no way in Hell this would look appropriate to a single soul who witnessed it.

Mr. D ran out of his office. Clearly, he wasn't expecting guests either.

"Go hide," he whispered, fear clearly written on his face. He obviously had the same thoughts that I did.

We were fucked if someone saw me standing in his living room, especially dressed the way I was.

I grabbed my books and did exactly as he ordered, quickly making my way to his office. Once I got inside, I still worried about being caught if for some reason they walked in. What if someone saw me enter? What if they wanted to search his apartment? What if it was a friend who walked about his house freely? I had no idea who was at the door, and I needed to prepare for the worst.

I saw a slatted wooden door in his office, and figured it was the closet. Hearing Mr. D open the front door, I knew I had to act fast. Juggling the books in my arms, I opened his closet and tried to enter, but he had it packed solid with boxes and storage containers. Realizing hiding in a closet was still a good idea, I bolted to his bedroom. Opening his closet, I entered, and squeezed myself to the furthest corner beneath his suits, his shirts, his hanging slacks, and sat next to all his shoes. Because of the slats in the door, the light from the room shone into the closet. Peeking through the slats, I could see his bed, his dresser, and another sliding glass door that I knew connected with the front balcony that was cracked open with a small breeze blowing in.

I was breathing so hard that I worried about being heard. Closing my mouth and concentrating on inhaling and exhaling through my nose, I closed my eyes and listened closely.

I could hear muffled voices but couldn't make out the words exactly. All I could tell was that the other voice was a female's. There also wasn't any shouting or sounds of aggression, so at least I knew that whoever was visiting wasn't here on bad terms or because they knew I was here. At least that was what I hoped.

I waited.

And waited.

And just as I considered getting out of the closet to go see if the guest had left because it had become quiet, I heard footsteps. I was embarrassed to have Mr. D find me in his closet, but I'd explain that I was taking the extra precaution just in case...

Just in case...

With my hand closed around the doorknob about to turn it, I saw Mr. D entering his room walking backwards with a woman pushing him toward the bed, kissing him. She already had his shirt off and was yanking at the button of his pants. Releasing the knob, I sank back down to the floor.

He was far more muscular than I had imagined with a chiseled stomach, but what was even more shocking was that tattoos covered both of his upper arms, his pecs, and he had a full back piece. The tattoos were only visible on the parts of his body he could hide with a suit. All business on the outside, but beneath the expensive material and a tie was an ink-covered canvas of perfection.

"Shelly, come on…" he said between the kissing. "I told you… I have a lot of work I need to get done tonight."

I watched how Mr. D's eyes darted around the room looking for me and a flicker of relief when he didn't see me.

"That's why I'm here," Shelly said, not stopping her sexual advances. "I know how you hate all the board members." She kept kissing him and lowering her lips to his neck and collarbone. "Except me, that is. And I'm not taking no for an answer."

"I have to get ready for the meeting tomorrow."

"You're always finding excuses not to be with me, lately. A girl could develop a complex."

"Shelly…" Mr. D softly pushed her back and walked over to the sliding glass door, trying to casually look outside for signs of me, but Shelly simply walked up behind him and began to practically hump his leg as she yanked her dress up over her head revealing she was wearing nothing beneath it but a pair of black panties that barely covered her firm ass.

"I'm not asking for anything but a fuck. I thought you were down for casual fun."

"You know the meeting tomorrow is important."

"Shh," she nearly purred. "You're entitled to a break."

Mr. D closed the slider, spun around and kissed her, fondling her bare breasts, as he led her away from the glass. I had a pretty good feeling he believed I was outside hiding on the deck, and by how hard he was trying to distract her and get her away from the balcony, he didn't want this Shelly chick discovering me.

"Give me a raincheck, and I'll make it up to you," Mr. D said as he quickly bent down and picked her dress up from the floor.

"Oh live a little, Drew. You work too much." Shelly pushed him against the edge of the bed, forcing him to sit on it.

She took the opportunity and quickly unfastened his pants completely and, without warning, pulled out his penis. I watched him quickly look at the slider, no doubt fearful that I would be able to see what was going on.

He clearly had no idea I was in the closet.

My breath caught in my throat as my heart skipped a beat. I knew I should look away. I was invading their personal space, and his personal... I was watching his dick as she began stroking it up and down with her hand.

I wasn't a virgin, but I was far from what I would consider experienced. No way could I be as aggressive and sexual as this woman was being. She was confident in every move she made, and she had one goal... to fuck Mr. D.

She kneeled between his legs and looked up at him with a wicked glint in her eyes.

"Let me take some of that stress away from you," she said as she kissed the head of his dick. "You know you like when I kiss you here." She pressed her lips to his hard flesh once again, following it with a swipe of her tongue.

"Shelly..."

"Drew..." She licked his full length, and I observed every sensual second of it. "You know every woman around that conference table tomorrow will want to fuck the infamous Drew Dawson. But only I will have. I want to know that some of your cum is still inside of me as we discuss budgets." She swirled her tongue along the head of his cock and giggled. "Come on... let's have a little fun in that knowledge."

Mr. D closed his eyes as she lowered her mouth along the entire length of his shaft. Up and down, her head bobbed. He moaned, took hold of her hair, and in a moment of strength and resistance, pulled her face away from his hard and glistening cock.

I couldn't stop watching.

It was so wrong. Twisted even. And yet, my eyes were glued to the scene before me.

I could see the discomfort on Mr. D's face as he was trying his damnedest to fight the woman off, but it was clear his hard dick had something else in mind. And I couldn't help but feel the same way as this Shelly woman. I didn't want to see this erotic movie come to an end.

I wanted more.

So, so much more.

My pussy throbbed even as my heart beat in fear, and I was two seconds away from touching myself as I spied on my principal getting a blow job in his bedroom.

My mind screamed. Everything was so wrong about this situation, but my body didn't care. It reacted more than it had ever done so before. Sinful thoughts of wanting to see more of Mr. D were flooding every rational sense inside.

I wanted to watch him fuck her.

I wanted to watch and pretend it was me.

"I need to get to work. I mean it. I can't do this right now. I'm sorry, but it's getting late, and I have a lot to do," he said, not releasing her hair and giving her a stern and uncompromising stare as he tugged her head back so she was forced to look into his eyes. "I'll make it up to you, but for now, I need you to leave."

She sighed loudly but nodded. He released her hair and she stood up and then reached for her dress.

"You better," she said with a pout. "I expect dinner *and* multiple orgasms as your way of an apology."

"Deal," he said, tucking his dick away from view and fastening his pants as he stood up from the bed. He stole a glance at the balcony again.

It was the first time I stopped staring at his crotch, and a part of me had wished he hadn't fought her from continuing on.

"Come on," he gave her a quick kiss, "I'll walk you out."

And just as quickly as they had entered the room, they had left. I considered leaving the closet and running through the slider since that was where Mr. D thought I was, but I was too afraid. What if they entered again just as I was crossing the room? They could change their mind and decide they wanted to have sex after all.

I remained in place, listening. It wasn't long before I heard the front door close, then the sound of footsteps in the hallway approaching the bedroom door. Mr. D entered and rushed straight to the slider and opened the door wide. He walked outside, looked left and right, then when he didn't see me, he walked to the railing and looked down as if I was courageous enough to jump.

Maybe I should have.

Taking a steadying breath, I stood, opened the door to the closet, and rubbed the fabric of Mr. D's shirt down my thighs to make sure I was completely decent. Well... as decent as you can be while wearing no panties and just having watched your principal get sucked off by a nearly naked woman.

"Jesus! Corrine," he said, as I startled him. "I thought you were hiding out here."

I pointed to the closet, feeling the heat from my face, and from my pussy, unite. "I was in there."

He looked at the closet, then the bed, then me. "Fuck. Did you..." He ran his hands through his hair and took a long pause. "I'm sorry. I was trying to get rid of her without making it totally obvious something was wrong."

I shook my head. "It's not your fault."

He looked back at the bed as his face turned a shade of pink. "Did you see—fuck." He cleared his throat. "I apologize."

I gave a weak smile, desperate to leave the room. Stepping back into my hiding place, I retrieved my things before turning around. "No problem. I'm the one who's sorry. I shouldn't be here getting in the way of you and your girlfriend's evening."

"She's not my girlfriend. She's just someone who I —" He shook his head and walked over to where I awkwardly stood. He placed his hand on my lower back and guided me out of the room. "Why don't we just get back to what we were doing. I'm sure you have homework, and I have to work."

I was never more grateful to have the conversation changed, but as he led me out of the room and down the hall, I wondered if he could feel that I had no panties on. Would he feel that there was no fabric seam beneath his fingers? And because I had no panties on, I wondered if it was obvious just how wet that entire voyeur situation had made me.

I glanced down and saw that his still hard dick tented his pants, and I realized that we would both end this evening highly aroused but with no way to quench the thirst.

7

Mr. D

I needed to jack off.

Even though I had been trying to distract my mind —and body—with work for the past hour, the fact remained... I needed to jack off.

But that wasn't something I was comfortable doing while a student of Black Mountain Academy worked on her homework in the other room. Especially since it was very likely that she had seen my fucking cock being sucked. Mortification would be an understatement, but there wasn't much that I could do about that fact either. All I cared about was that Shelly had no idea that Corrine was hiding in the closet, because that would have been disastrous. And if Corrine had truly witnessed everything I was pretty sure she had witnessed, then she would be just as embarrassed as I and want to keep it secret as well. And I highly doubted she wanted to discuss it any more than I wanted to.

It was getting late, and I needed to get some sleep. I also knew that Corrine had to be tired, and I hadn't set her up yet with a place to sleep. Going to the closet in the office, I pulled out extra blankets and a pillow and then made my way to the front room and—

Fucking hell...

Corrine was lying on her stomach on the couch reading a book. Completely innocent except for the fact that the shirt she wore—my shirt—had risen so far up her thighs, that I could see the lower part of her ass. Her toned, smooth, and perfectly touchable ass.

No way was she wearing panties. Possibly a thong... but no fabric covered her ass.

My cock—that had never truly recovered from earlier—twitched and hardened fully at the sight.

She didn't hear me enter the room because she had earphones in, and by the little tap of her foot, was most likely listening to music. This allowed me to truly take in her full beauty... her totally luscious, and extremely desirable beauty.

If she were mine, I would be straddling her right then and there and taking her from behind, driving my cock deep inside of her as she screamed out my —

What the fuck was wrong with me?

She was a student of Black Mountain Academy!

Yes, she was *of age*, but I wasn't that guy. No fucking way.

I wasn't that guy!

Go to bed, Drew. Go to bed. Go to fucking bed.

Trying to ignore my hard on, I walked around the couch so she could see me. Once I did, she practically jumped right off the cushions. She pulled out her earphones with eyes wide as saucers.

"I'm sorry. I didn't mean to scare you," I said, placing the blankets and pillow on the edge of the couch.

"It doesn't take much these days," she said as she sat up straight, hiding the curve of her bare ass that had made me lose all sense of reason. "I feel like I don't know how to *not* be jumpy."

"I think you have a good reason."

"Do I?" she asked, looking up at me with sadness dancing in the depths of her eyes. "I feel like I'm losing my mind. Why would I have a stalker? It makes sense that my mother would. But why me? Maybe it's all in my head."

"Someone came in and opened those doors. No way you could make that up. I saw it with my own eyes."

"Yeah, but why?"

"I don't know, but we'll get to the bottom of it. Tomorrow is a new day, and I'm going to get hold of your mother somehow because, at the very least, she needs to help deal with this and your needed security."

Corrine rolled her eyes and gave a half-hearted laugh. "Good luck with that."

"Let's get some sleep," I said. I reached for her hand to help her off the couch. "You can have my room, and I'll take the couch. I wish I had an air mattress or something to set up in the spare bedroom, but—"

"No way," she interrupted, shaking her head. "I can't take your bed. I won't."

"I'm a gentleman, Corrine," I said with a little bow. "It's my duty."

"I've already put you out so much tonight. Absolutely not." She took the pillow and the blankets and started to make up the couch. "I insist."

I was too tired to argue, and my dick was still hard, so being in her presence while she was wearing nothing but my t-shirt wasn't a wise idea either.

"All right, well if you need anything..."

"Mr. D," she said quickly as I began to walk away. "Can you make sure the house is closed up? I would but I'm not sure..."

I gave a reassuring smile. "I locked everything the minute Shelly left, but yes, I'll double-check. No worries."

I already knew all doors and windows were locked, but I went and checked each one because I knew Corrine's eyes were on me as I did so, and the small gesture would go far with her. Poor girl needed to feel some sense of safety.

Once I was done, I went and dropped down on the coffee table, leaning forward to where she sat on the couch and patted her arm. "It's going to be all right. I promise. You shouldn't have to go through this alone, and tomorrow we'll come up with a plan."

Tears welled in her eyes, but she didn't allow them to fall. I saw the resistance to show weakness, but knew she desperately needed to be held. Proper student principal etiquette be damned, I moved to the edge of the couch and pulled her into my arms, holding her close.

It was likely that I was the first form of physical contact and comfort she'd had in a long time because she instantly pressed her weight into me, nuzzled her head into my shoulder and clung to my clothing with her fingers. She needed this. I could feel it. I could sense it. And the poor girl deserved it.

Should I have pulled away?

Maybe.

But right now, this frightened woman needed comfort. She needed to know she wasn't alone anymore. I hadn't volunteered for this position, but there sure as hell wasn't anyone else who was standing in line to fill the spot.

"I'm tired of being scared. I hate being alone. I'm even more tired of feeling insane." Her muffled voice broke my heart. She held on to me with tight fists, and I could tell she didn't want to break our connection anytime soon.

I rubbed her back and tried not to focus on the smell of her hair—fruits and tea tree. "Just try to get some sleep. I promise you that we'll try to come up with a solution tomorrow."

She backed away from my embrace and swiped at the tears in her eyes. "I haven't slept through a night in forever. I don't even know what a good night's rest feels like anymore."

I repositioned the pillow at the farthest end of the couch and patted it. "Lie down."

She did so, and once she was stretched out, I covered her with one of the blankets and folded the remaining one at her feet in case she got cold. I then walked over to the kitchen, filled a glass with water, and brought it to the coffee table within easy reach if she got thirsty. I didn't want her to have to fumble in the dark in the middle of the night.

"I can sit in this chair and wait until you fall asleep," I said, willing to do whatever it took to make her feel safe.

She smiled warmly as she pulled the blanket up under her chin and rolled to her side so she could stare at me. "Thank you, but I'll be fine." She giggled which was a welcomed sound for me. "I don't think having my principal sit here and watch me try to fall asleep will help with my insomnia."

I moved over to my favorite leather chair, reclined back in it, and smirked. "I think we've crossed the line of being more than just student and principal, wouldn't you say?"

She giggled again as she burrowed her cheek into the pillow. "What? You don't share your Raiders shirt with your other students?"

"Just the special ones," I said as I made myself comfortable. I had no intentions of leaving her alone in this room until I was confident she would be able to fall asleep.

"Special? Does that mean that I'm out of detention?"

"Ahh, playing dirty, I see. Trying to get what you want when I'm tired and defenseless." I gave a wink. "That depends if you plan on being honest with me on why you've been late and missed so much school since arriving here."

She remained silent but I could see that she was studying me, considering if she could trust me with the information.

"I think it's the least I'm owed," I added. "And I'm also not going to judge you if that's what you're afraid of."

"I think I have OCD or something," she said softly, her gaze dropping to the carpeted floor.

"Explain," I prodded, not giving up on what could be a very difficult conversation.

She looked back up at me. "I keep every door in my house closed. Every single door. But I then doubt if I truly closed them all. I double-check over and over again. I go upstairs, then downstairs, then upstairs again. I close the windows, check them again and again. I make sure all the curtains are drawn and won't allow even a sliver of space between the fabric. And just when I feel I have the house sealed up tight... I repeat the entire process again. And sometimes... again. It gets to the point where I can spend half the day obsessing. And then when I finally get the courage to leave the house, I have to run to my car. And sometimes I worry I'm being followed so I drive around in circles... not going to school." She repositioned herself so that she was leaning up on her elbow, clearly growing agitated with the memories. "I feel I'm two seconds from being committed sometimes, and my school attendance is my last concern."

A huge wave of disappointment hit me in the gut like a freight train. I was disgusted with myself. All my training had taught me that not all students were the same. I couldn't just rule with an iron fist and not observe. I needed to listen and be aware that some behavioral issues were due to outside factors, and here I was failing to observe this with Corrine. In Oakland, I prided myself on being able to work with troubled youth. But here at Black Mountain Academy, I just forgot all that. Why? Because they were rich?

I'd fucked up.

Corrine was calling for help, and my answer was simply giving her detention. Jesus, I'd really fucked up.

"I think you're afraid," I said softly. "Which is to be expected. Someone's messing with you, and whether it's dangerous or not, we don't know. But I don't blame you one bit for doing what you do. But we're going to put a stop to it." She released the breath she seemed to be holding. "Did you have these issues in L.A.? Is that why you were held back a year?"

"Yes, and no. I always felt like I was being watched, and in many ways I was. Being the daughter of Candy Parker wasn't easy. Photographers camped outside our house, so I just assumed my uneasy feeling was that. I didn't really feel it was a single person watching me until I made the move. I was pretty sure my move wasn't worthy of paparazzi following me here. Plus, there were staff in the L.A. house so I never truly felt like I wasn't under some sort of watchful eye. It took being alone to feel that someone was *really* watching."

"And being held back a year in school?"

"Long story," she said softly. "Not one I really want to discuss. But I was held back in fourth grade. Not high school. Not because of this stalker guy."

Fair enough. She had already opened up enough, far more than I'd expected, and I didn't want to disrupt her safe space talking with me by being too pushy.

She yawned which was a good sign. She then repositioned herself on her pillow and asked, "So about that detention?"

I chuckled. "Consider it rescinded." I stifled a yawn myself, not wanting her to feel like I was being *put out* as she said. "But you aren't going home tomorrow until we reach your mom or figure something out. So, come to my office after school if you haven't heard from me all day. Deal?"

She nodded. "Deal." She pointed to the hallway. "Go to bed, Mr. D." She gave a reassuring smile. "I know you're as tired as I am."

"Did you get your uniform dry?" For some reason, I wasn't ready to leave her.

"Yes."

"Feel free to use whatever I have in the shower tomorrow. There are clean towels under the sink."

"Ooh, so I get to smell like Mr. D all day tomorrow. Gotta love it."

Her joking around with me did bring up something that I needed to address again. "Corrine, about all this—"

"Don't worry. I'm not going to tell a single soul. I know how it looks. I know how much trouble this could get you in, and frankly any drama right now goes far beyond my mental ability to cope."

"I'm going to take you to school, but maybe I should drop you off a block away. For both our sakes. I'm sure it won't look cool to your peers to be arriving with me."

"I couldn't care less what any of them think about me, but yes, I agree."

"And I promise you, it will get better. You aren't alone anymore."

I didn't make promises lightly, and I rarely tried to raise false expectations, but this was one promise I would make. No, Corrine was not a troubled youth in Oakland involved with gangs, or poverty, but she was someone in need. It was my job to help her, and I planned to take it seriously.

I got out of my chair and stared down at her. I didn't want to leave her but knew we both needed sleep. "Goodnight, Corrine."

"Goodnight, Mr. D. Thank you."

"If you need anything..."

"I know where to find you."

8

At least I was on time for school today.

No doors to close. No need to run to a car.

It was the first day in a long time that I actually felt somewhat human and rested as I got ready to enter history class. I even had my homework done thanks to Mr. D playfully nagging me to do it.

This was what normal felt like, and I liked it.

"Corrine!" Kevin called from the west-wing hallway. I stopped and waited for him to get close. "I've been looking for you all day. Where have you been?"

"Just trying to get to classes on time and catching up with work. I'm on thin ice."

"I swung by your house this morning to pick you up just in case you couldn't get a car working and was too stubborn to call me for help. But you weren't home."

"Yeah... I slept someplace else last night."

"You did? Why? Where?"

"Crazy story, but I couldn't stay there." I hated to lie to Kevin because that just wasn't the kind of friends we were, and I never had to lie before. "I stayed at a bed and breakfast."

But I didn't have a choice. I couldn't risk him slipping up and telling someone. I didn't think he'd judge me, but he did have loose lips, especially since he was trying so hard to sit at the cool kid's table. Having some juicy gossip could aid him in that quest.

He tilted his head and narrowed his eyes. "Okay..." He waited, and when I refused to say anything more, he thankfully moved on. "There's a football game tonight. Wanna go?"

I shrugged. "Friday night football's not really my jam." I didn't think it was Kevin's either, but I understood he was trying really hard for that fresh start. He was simply playing the game that I sucked at. "Don't worry about me. I have to deal with some stuff with the house and need to get hold of my mom this weekend somehow."

"Anything I can help with?"

I shook my head, glanced at my phone to see the bell was about to ring. The last thing I needed was to be late to history class. Mr. Monati was a stickler for time and wouldn't hesitate for a second to mark me tardy, and Mr. D would lose his mind. After how nice he had been toward me, I really didn't want to piss him off or make him feel I was trying to push the boundaries or take advantage.

"I'm good. Just need to reach my mother. School needs it. I need it." I shrugged again and started walking toward class. Kevin walked with me, but I knew he would change directions soon since we didn't have history together. "Time for me to try to hunt down the maternal figure."

"Yeah, good luck with that. Try to find mine while you're at it too." He dodged a crowd of laughing girls and waved at me as he went to his class. "I'll check up on you this weekend. We can hang out."

I waved him off and gave a nod even though I seriously doubted we would. I wasn't really a hanging-out type of gal either. Frankly, I was pretty damn boring.

History was one of my favorite classes. I wasn't great at remembering dates, but the rest of the information I found fascinating. I think it helped that I had actually traveled to many of the places we studied about, so it made it all more real and not just facts from a textbook. I remembered the smells, the weather, the appearance of structures from a time long ago. But even in a class that normally held my attention, I was distracted. It wasn't hard to know why that was.

It was Mr. D.

I had seen his dick.

And we didn't discuss it again, even though we both knew I saw it.

And not only had I seen his dick, but I wanted to see it again. The sinful thoughts that hadn't left my mind since, were becoming my new obsession. I could still smell him from our car ride this morning. This morning when he'd come out of his bedroom after he'd showered, smelling like expensive cologne, in a fresh suit and tie, I'd nearly melted.

He was gorgeous.

He smelled good.

And his eyes were on me.

He had a way of making me feel special... looked after... cared for.

I had actually slept through the night which is unheard of for me. I couldn't remember the last time I did. Granted, it was nice having someone there with me who offered protection if need be, but there was more to it. I had actually opened up and had a real conversation with someone. He genuinely seemed to listen and care. And it felt like a million pounds had been lifted from my shoulders.

"Miss Parker," Mr. Donati said, snapping me from my thoughts. "Mr. D just called asking to see you in his office."

Ignoring the snickers and trying to not focus on how everyone watched me pack up my stuff, I quickly left the classroom. Great. Now everyone would be wondering what I did to deserve a summons to the principal's office.

I had to wait in the row of chairs where all the bad boys and girls sat awaiting their punishments when I got there because Mr. D was in with a student. It forced me to have to sit next to Bobby Jackson which I hated. He, however, seemed to like the company because he kept trying to talk to me and the secretary kept telling him to sit there and be quiet. Yes, we were sitting in the office together, but I was not like him. I was not a troublemaker. I didn't belong next to him...

But, in all reality, I was causing a lot of trouble for Mr. D...

So, I really was just as guilty as Bobby.

Mr. D finally exited his office with a red-faced boy I didn't recognize. If looks could kill, the boy would have for sure murdered Mr. D, but Mr. D seemed unfazed.

"Mr. Moran will be dealing with you, Mr. Jackson. I advise you to sit there and keep your mouth shut until he does." He looked at me. "Corrine..." He motioned for me to follow him into his office.

I did so, wondering if I was in trouble. Mr. D seemed to be in a foul mood, and the last thing I wanted to be was on the receiving end of it.

"Close the door," he ordered when I entered. "Have a seat."

This wasn't the man who had practically tucked me in last night and sat with me until I was ready to fall asleep. Nor was this the man who had made me a bagel with cream cheese and gave me too strong coffee for the road. I didn't know why I expected him to still be... friendly... at school, but he seemed far from it.

"We've been trying to reach your mother all day." His jaw flexed and his tone was flat. "I even spoke to her manager Bill who, frankly, is an asshole."

I smirked, nodded, but remained silent.

He sighed and pressed the ridge of his nose between his finger and thumb. "It's been a long day, and I had hoped we would have at least gotten somewhere." He leaned back in his chair and studied me for what felt like an awkward eternity. "I'm not sure how to handle this. I know you said to not get the police involved, but I really don't see what else we can do."

"Please don't," I began to beg. "And even if you do, I don't think it will help. I tried that. It did nothing."

"We could get you a bodyguard, but I don't really feel like it's my place to do so. Plus, we would need to interview, and it's not something that can be done overnight. Because of who your mother is, I know we need to be careful about vetting all who come into your life. We don't want to risk them selling information to the media about you. And frankly, I'm not comfortable making decisions without some input from your mother."

"I'm nineteen," I reminded. "I can make these decisions without her."

He nodded, crossed his arms and said, "I've taken that into consideration too. But it's her money. And you're right. You are legally allowed to do all this yourself, but you shouldn't have to. I think you've been alone long enough. And I made a promise to you that I plan to keep."

"I'm sorry this has been such a pain."

"It's not your fault that your mother is—" He paused as if reconsidering what he'd been about to say. "So, we have an issue we need to address now."

"Issue?"

"I'm obviously not going to just let you walk out that door and go back to a house where your safety could be at risk. You also don't have a car, so you'd need a ride anyway. You don't have anywhere to go except a bed and breakfast which we ruled out last night. Which leaves *me*."

"I would never ask you—"

"Yes, well..." he interrupted. "We don't have a lot of options right now, and since it's been a long day, and I don't have enough energy left to address alternate solutions, you'll be staying on my couch again." He paused. "If that's what you want to do, that is. I also don't want you to feel that this is coming from Mr. D, your principal, giving you an order you have to follow. But this is coming from someone who cares... a friend."

I could have sat there and argued. I could have tried to convince him he didn't have to worry about me. I could have even lied and told him I was completely fine and would be okay going home. But the thought of going into that empty house terrified me. I'd never been the type of girl to need her *mommy*, but I did feel pretty damn abandoned and alone right now, and Mr. D was offering a lifeline.

"I appreciate the offer. I do. Thank you."

Appearing satisfied with my answer, he leaned down and picked up his briefcase and began loading it with manila folders and notebooks.

"Okay, good. Go get your stuff and wait for me after school in detention." He looked up and smiled. "Consider detention back on. I need you to hang out somewhere until I can leave. I have a meeting I need to run to, and then I'll give you a ride to the house to pick up some clothing and essentials. Plan for a couple of days. It's not an ideal situation, but until we get hold of someone who can reach your mother or at least step in, we'll just wait it out."

I nodded, not minding detention. I got it. I couldn't exactly hang out in his office spinning in his chair as I snooped in the files of classmates.

"Corrine..." he began and stared me directly in the eyes. "We need to handle this delicately. You can agree that this won't look good to others."

"I completely agree," I said. "Down low." I hated to use the words "our secret" because that made it seem somehow wrong and forbidden.

I might have had improper thoughts, but they were mine alone. Mr. D had done nothing even slightly inappropriate... even though deep down the fantasy of him doing more to me was present. But it was just a fantasy.

A fantasy I would take to my grave.

He stood up from his desk. "Okay, good. This is a temporary solution to a messed up situation." He nodded to the door. "I'm late for my meeting, but I'll see you soon. We can then figure out what we want to do for dinner." He gave a warm smile. "Roomie."

9

CORRINE

Maybe I should move back to L.A. At least there were people there. Granted, they were housekeepers, landscapers, and stupid Bill, but at least there were other humans.

But instead, here I was, pulling up in front of my house with Mr. D all because of open doors. Had I lost my mind?

Was I taking advantage of Mr. D's kindness all because I was afraid of the Boogie Man?

Yes.

Was I using him because I had never felt so alone in my life?

Yes to that as well.

Mr. D stopped the car, got out, walked around to my side, and opened the door for me. My mother had taught me to allow a man to open the door for you, but until Mr. D, no one ever had. My mother would most definitely approve of his old-school manners.

"Pack a suitcase for several days," he said. "Even if we reach your mom, we don't know how long it will take her to get back to the States from wherever she is."

I fumbled for my keys and unlocked the door half expecting someone to jump out and grab me. I opened the door slowly and was pleased to at least find the house the way we had left it.

Mr. D glanced around and said, "I'll walk around and make sure everything's locked up while you pack."

I quickly ran upstairs, and when I entered my room, a scream erupted from the depths of my chest, vibrating every muscle in my body.

Painted in red paint on the wall above my headboard was the word:

WHORE

I needed Mr. D. I needed him now.

"What's wrong?" Mr. D bellowed as he charged up the stairs. "Corrine!"

"In here," I said weakly, blinking against the graffiti, not sure how to handle myself with Mr. D and what was on my wall.

When Mr. D entered the room, he froze in his tracks. "Jesus Christ."

He reached for a pair of scissors off my desk and held them in his hand in a defensive pose. "Wait right here," he commanded as he quickly looked in my closet, under my bed, and then ran out in the hallway to check the rest of the rooms.

Knowing he would want us out of the house as quickly as possible, I reached for my suitcase and began throwing clothing and shoes inside it without much thought. It helped that I had to wear a uniform to school, so I tossed in several different uniform shirts and skirts so I wouldn't have to keep wearing the same one. It was also the weekend, so I added a bunch of casual outfits as well.

"I'm sorry," Mr. D said as he entered the room with his phone to his ear. "I'm calling the police. This has crossed a line that I'm no longer comfortable not notifying the police about. There's actual proof that someone has been in your house now. They need to know."

I sighed in defeat, but sort of agreed. At least I wouldn't be the crazy girl saying I just felt like someone was watching me. And the door thing would be hard for anyone to understand. But dripping red paint with a foul word painted on my bedroom wall was pretty hard to argue against. And I couldn't be accused of doing it myself because I had an air-tight alibi with school and being in detention.

It didn't take long for the police to arrive, especially since Mr. D had told the dispatcher he wasn't sure if the invader were still on the property or not. We had made our way to the kitchen while we waited. My packed suitcase was at the door, because regardless of what the police said, I was still leaving. Mr. D had exchanged my scissors for a kitchen knife, and I wondered if anyone would be foolish enough to take this man on.

He was cool and collected, but there was a fierce energy surrounding him as well. I felt protected in his presence—even in this house.

"We've checked everywhere, and we're confident that whoever entered the house has left," the policeman said.

"I would suggest having someone stay with you tonight," his partner added, looking at me, "since you said you live alone. We'll have an extra patrol drive by the house, but since you said you have an alarm system, this person clearly knows how to not get caught. I wouldn't be alone for a while if you can help it."

"She's staying elsewhere," Mr. D piped in. "But since this isn't Miss Parker's first complaint, I'm hoping *this one* gets taken seriously."

The police officer nodded, reached out and shook Mr. D's hand and then nodded toward me. "I'm sorry you've had to experience this. There are some crazy people out there. Don't hesitate to call if you even get a hint he's returned."

Mr. D escorted them out the door, and I stood in amazement that I seemed to not be the joke of the police department. They actually took the call seriously, although it was hard to deny the big *WHORE* painted in blood red on my wall.

"Okay, you ready to get out of here?" Mr. D asked.

I couldn't have been more ready. "All packed."

"Did you get everything you need for school? Laptop? Books?"

I smiled, once again finding all the different faces Mr. D wore around me funny. Protector, guardian, friend, principal, and sex symbol—the last one being one that I would only admit to myself. "I got it all."

I handed the keys to Mr. D so he could be the one to lock up. I liked his take-charge attitude and how he seemed to make everything feel good, and warm. But in the corner of my eye, something moved in the far-off bushes.

I froze, and Mr. D sensed my fear.

"What's wrong?" he asked, looking in the same direction I was.

I shook my head, pretty sure it was just a squirrel or something non-threatening considering the police had just left.

"Do you see anything?" he asked.

"I saw something move, but nothing now."

He took me by the hand and led me to the car, keeping his eyes on the area. If there was someone hiding, I seriously doubted anyone would have the balls to jump out and mess with Mr. D. His facial expression was enough to scare anyone. He wasn't messing around.

"I know you didn't want to involve the police," he said as we were driving off the property. "But we need the record. You're right in the fact that we may never catch the sicko messing with you, but if he ever slips up, we need a paper trail to really nail him."

"Do you think he knows I'm with you?" I asked. "That's why he painted *WHORE*. Maybe he thinks you and I are... well, you know."

"Possibly," Mr. D said as he kept his eyes on the road, but then looked into the rearview mirror. "Do you have any idea who could be doing this? Any enemies? Any past boyfriends you did wrong?"

"I don't have any enemies, and no real boyfriends to speak of."

He quickly glanced at me. "No boyfriends? Come on. You're a beautiful girl, and I seriously doubt you've lived the life of a nun."

"I'm not claiming to be a nun. But no real relationships in my life. Not like you think or would define as a boyfriend anyway. Have I hooked up with a few? Yeah," I said, feeling my face heat over the fact that I was admitting to having sex with men of my past to my principal. Also... Mr. D called *me* beautiful. "But nothing serious. I doubt anyone cares enough about me—hate or love—to follow me to Black Mountain and watch my every move."

"You said you weren't sure if the stalking started in Black Mountain or L.A."

"Well, no one painted *WHORE* on my wall in L.A., but you're right. I have no idea when this truly started and why."

"Has anyone had a crush on you? Made a move on you that you rejected?" he asked. I had already answered these questions to the police, but I didn't mind answering them again.

I shook my head. "I think you're giving my sexual prowess far too much credit. I'm what you would call the classic wallflower. I prefer to keep to myself."

"What about that kid Kevin you're friends with? Is he secretly lusting after you?"

I laughed. "Oh my god, no. There is nothing between Kevin and me, and never has been. There's been plenty of opportunity and no moves made. We come from the same dysfunctional world and bonded that way. If anything, the guy would feel for me. Who knows, he could have a stalker of his own. He's used to the paparazzi, the craziness, and he just wants a normal life. He's desperately searching for it and camping outside my house would really put a damper on the social life he's working so hard on. I really don't think it's someone who finds me desirable. I'm just not that interesting."

"Maybe you think so, but as I hunted down your mother today, I saw a lot of old magazine photos with you in them. Paparazzi loved you just as much as your mother. You didn't tell me you acted in a movie before."

My stomach coiled. "Against my will. I hated every second of it, but my mother and Bill made me. They thought I'd be perfect for the role, and at first I liked the extra attention I was getting from my mother, but like with all things, she got bored. I, on the other hand, got stuck living and going to school on set. Miserable wouldn't be a strong enough word to describe my dip into the movie biz."

"But actors get stalkers. It's normal. So, maybe yours comes from that time period."

"Maybe... or from all the parties I've been to. My mother went on a party host kick for a while and had one almost every night. There were constant people flowing in and out of the house. A lot of drugs, sex, and creeps."

"Does anyone stand out from the parties? Someone who made a sexual pass? Someone who gave you a bad feeling?"

I chuckled. "I've lost count. Frankly, there was a sea of men who got too grabby. Power, wealth, and stardom gives many a free pass."

"And let me guess... your mother did nothing."

I didn't answer. Did I need to? Mr. D was slowly getting the picture of my life.

"So, what do you want for dinner?" Mr. D asked. I had never been more grateful for a change of subject as I was right then.

"Whatever you want. I'll cook. It's the least that I can do."

He took his focus away from the road and looked at me with raised eyebrows. "You cook?"

"Well... no. But I could try."

Mr. D laughed loudly. "I would rather we not experiment tonight. I'm starving. How about we swing by this great Mexican restaurant down the mountain and get takeout?"

"Sounds great," I said, noticing how we were once again getting dinner someplace not in the heart of Black Mountain.

I didn't blame the man one bit.

"Mr. D..." I said softly. "Could you get in a lot of trouble for doing this for me? Could you lose your job?"

He licked his lips, tensed his shoulders and nodded. "It wouldn't look good. There's no way around how this appears. Legally I can't get into trouble because you aren't a child. But the board would rip me to shreds." He glanced over at me. "But regardless, I make my own decisions. I've never been one to march to the beat of conformity. If it gets out that I stepped in to help you, I'll stand by my decision. Fuck anyone who tries to judge me for it."

"I promise I won't tell a soul."

"I appreciate that," he said. "But at the same time, you aren't my dirty little secret, Corrine. Don't ever feel that way. I'm here with you because I choose to be. I want to help. I've given a lot of thought to this and just how much involvement I want to engage in. I'm following my gut. And we aren't doing anything I'm uncomfortable with." He turned onto the highway leading us out of Black Mountain. "But at the same time, if this situation ever makes *you* feel uncomfortable, I want you to tell me. I know it's weird. I'm sure you didn't exactly want to spend your Friday night getting Mexican food with your principal."

I gave a small giggle, but it was just to hide my true feelings.

The truth...

I wouldn't want to be anywhere else.

"But I don't want you to lose your job," I said, growing serious again.

"Then it's not a job worth keeping." He shrugged his shoulder. "Between you and me, I'm not sure it really is."

"You don't like being a principal at Black Mountain Academy?"

"I thought I would. I'm trying to find the joy in it. Harder than expected," he admitted.

"Why did you want to be a principal?"

"To make a difference," he answered quickly. "But I'm not sure I actually have."

I opened my mouth to tell him just how much of a difference he'd made with me, but decided that confessions could happen another time.

10

CORRINE

I always wondered what normal felt like. I always had assumed that the definition of normal was different for everyone, but I most certainly knew I had never experienced it.

Not like now.

A normal night sitting on the couch with someone watching a movie. I never did things like this growing up or even now. My mother would never waste an evening doing such a thing, and anytime I would want to watch TV, it was alone. I didn't date guys... not in the normal way. So, sitting on a couch side by side with a man was a completely new and foreign experience.

Normal.

Now I could define it for myself.

Mr. D was wearing gray sweats, a black t-shirt, and was barefoot. He leaned back on the couch with a beer in his hand, his feet resting on the coffee table, and he appeared so different than the principal at Black Mountain Academy.

And I was out of that damn uniform and in my own sweats. My mother would have been appalled that I sat with a man in attire anything less than put together. Sweats were a dirty word in our house. But again, my life was not normal.

Not like right now.

"Do you need another beer?" Mr. D asked as he stood up to get another one for himself.

"I'm good, thanks," I said, raising my half-full beer bottle. I sipped on it, not really liking the taste but wanting to do something as simple as sit on the couch watching a movie while drinking a beer.

And that's what we did. Sat, drank beer, and watched a movie.

Two normal people.

Doing a normal activity.

And I couldn't be happier.

"I don't know the last time I sat on a couch and binged movies," he said. He turned to face me and smiled. We were close enough that our legs touched, and I found myself focusing on that rather than the plot of the movie. "It's nice. I know this isn't exactly how you planned to spend your night, but I'm happy you're here."

"I haven't had a night like this before either," I admitted. "It's the best Friday night I can remember having." And it was.

Cozy, warm, in excellent company, and relaxed.

When the movie was over, Mr. D stood up and went to get the blankets from the spare room. When he walked out with them, I stopped him from speaking because I knew he'd offer to sleep on the couch again.

"I slept perfectly last night," I said. "I like your couch. It was the best sleep I've had in a long time."

He shook his head with a smirk. "My mother is rolling over in her grave right now." But he put the blankets and pillow on the couch and walked to the kitchen, turned the water on and got me a glass of water like he had last night.

Mr. D was going to tuck me in again.

I liked it.

"Are you tired, or do you need me to sit with you for bit?" he asked.

"I'm fine. I know you're tired." I gave him a big smile. "I'm good. I'll see you in the morning."

"Okay then, goodnight." He left my side, turned off the lights and left the room.

Would I have liked for him to stay?

Yes, very much so.

I had no doubt in my mind now.

Mr. D was freakin' hot and was the first guy to ever seem to actually care about me. He was there for me. I could count on him. His attention made me feel safe.

Safe...

Was I safe?

Was he safe?

What if something happened to him all because of me?

What if something went terribly wrong for the both of us?

I tossed and turned on the couch with all these awful thoughts going on in my head. Minutes turned to hours, and the good night's rest from before was now only a passing memory.

What if he got hurt? What if I got hurt? Obsession was a very dangerous thing, and we both could be at risk.

Were the doors closed tightly?

Did we block out all the bad, all the evil that could penetrate within this perfect and normal bubble I was in?

My head began to spin, my stomach churn. Voices entered my head, fighting with my sanity.

Not being able to remain silent in the dark anymore, I tiptoed to Mr. D's bedroom without really thinking through all the consequences of what that action could mean.

He could reject me.

He could kick me out of his house and never speak to me again.

He could ignore me like the rest of the world seemed to do.

Or he could hold me.

Maybe he'd tell me that everything would be all right, and that he would chase all the monsters away.

I had nothing to lose at this point but everything to gain.

Like a child sneaking into her parent's room for comfort after a nightmare, I innocently entered. I just needed to feel safe. I needed to not be alone. All other thoughts—thoughts of reason—vanished for mental preservation.

He didn't stir when I entered the room. Almost as if I were in a trance or sleepwalking, I padded to the empty side of the bed and crawled in beside him. My weight on the mattress woke him, and he turned, startled to see it was me in bed beside him. Not giving him the chance to say anything that would shatter my heart, I pressed my body against him and cuddled into his arms.

"Hold me," I whispered. "I'm afraid."

His body was warm, and his bare chest heated my icy skin. As he tightened his arms around me, I nearly exploded in joy when he kissed the top of my head.

"You don't need to be scared any longer. I'm not going to let anyone hurt you," he said in a low and gravelly voice.

I exhaled as he inhaled, and we shared the same air. I inched even closer, splaying my hands on his back so that he'd never be able to leave my side. If we could remain this way forever, I would never hear the voices of terror again. They'd lose all control over me. I'd win, and they would have to run to their hole in defeat. I felt safe. So, very safe. The madness inside silenced, and for the first time in maybe forever, my mind was quiet.

As I moved even closer, I felt the hardness between his legs, betraying his thoughts. True thoughts. Thoughts that I shared but tried so hard to hide from.

I was done hiding.

Taking my hand off his back, I moved it to the hardness and pressed, stroked, and circled my fingertips along the length of his shaft.

"Corrine," he whispered.

I ignored his voice. He didn't stop me. Maybe he wanted to, but he didn't, and I took that as my cue to continue on. I moved my head so I was burrowed against his neck. My lips were so close to his flesh that I kissed. Once, twice, and then a third. I continued to caress his covered cock, letting my intentions be known, but not being overly aggressive in my actions either.

His breathing deepened, but his body didn't tense. He remained in place as if he was anticipating my next move. So, I took this opportunity to run my fingertips to the edge of his boxers that he slept in and dipped them beneath the elastic band. My fingers made contact with skin, and I kept descending down until my palm brushed against hot flesh and my fingers curled to wrap around his dick. It was heavy, long, thick, and hard as steel. It was everything I imagined it would feel like when watching him with Shelly.

"We shouldn't," he said, but he didn't pull away as I caressed and teased.

He wanted this. I knew he did.

"If we don't stop now," he said, "we may not be able to."

"I don't want this to stop," I confessed as I moved my lips from his neck to his mouth.

He kissed me with lips of doubt.

I kissed him with lips of lust.

But he would change his mind soon.

I could feel the touch of his hand. The soft caress of my arm. He moved the stray hairs away from my face and was so close I could feel the warmth of his breath.

With the gentlest of touches, he placed his lips to mine with another kiss. Heat pumped through my veins and tiny jolts of pleasure sizzled through every nerve ending in my body. My eyes fluttered as his mouth conquered mine.

His kiss had woken an insanity that I had desperately tried to deny.

He woke up my crazy.

He woke up my reckless.

He woke up a siren determined to be heard.

I returned the kiss with a tiny moan as I wrapped my arms around his neck and pulled him closer, deeper to what had become my drug.

"Touch me," I said between our kissing. I danced my tongue with his which made me only want more. I craved all of him. Now. Right now.

Not waiting for him, I leaned up so I was sitting on my knees and lifted my shirt up over my head. His eyes watched every move I made. They were hungry but uncertain. I knew he wanted this, but the good angel on his shoulder was trying to convince him to stop.

I just needed to appeal to the devil on the other side.

I lowered my sweats next and tossed them to the side of the bed. Wearing nothing but pink panties, I straddled him as my eyes remained locked with his.

Yes, Mr. D. I want this.

This time when I lowered my mouth to kiss him, he was the one who pushed his tongue inside and deepened the kiss. He took hold of the back of my head and brought me even closer, silently telling me that he was now in control.

It was on.

We were both doing this.

I reached down to remove his shorts, and he assisted me in tossing them to join my clothes. He no longer wanted my panties getting in the way, so he quickly rid me of those as well.

Naked.

Ready.

Hungry.

Wet.

Yes, Mr. D. Yes.

Taking hold of my ass with both of his hands, he ground his cock into my pussy, stroking the fire as the flames inside my body grew higher.

"You sure you want this?" he asked, but I got the feeling it was a warning of what was to come, not an offer to stop.

I licked my lips and lowered my mouth to his again.

The tip of his dick touched the entrance to my pussy, and I knew this was it. He was going to fuck me, but just as I was getting prepared for the pressure and the spreading of me wide as he entered, he flipped me over onto my back and reached for the bedside table. Opening the drawer, he pulled out a condom, ripped it open with his teeth, and put it on with one smooth motion. There was nothing awkward or uncomfortable in his movements. This was a man. A true man who knew what he was doing.

Instead of mounting me and fucking, as I was ravenous for him to do, he ran his fingers along my stomach, tracing a sensual path to my breasts, and then back down to my pussy. He dipped his finger between the seam of my lips and found my clit, causing me to arch my back and moan.

Oh dear God.

"You are fucking beautiful, Corrine."

My face heated as the warmth in my body only intensified. His words were intoxicating, but his eyes gliding over my bare flesh were like a drug that made me higher than imaginable.

"I want to feel you inside of me," I nearly moaned.

"Tell me what you want again," he said as he thrust his finger inside of me.

I would have driven his entire hand inside of me if I could have when I pressed my hips to his palm, craving so much more.

"I want you."

"You want me to fuck this pussy?"

I nodded as I closed my eyes to try to calm my craze. I was about to orgasm and all he was doing was finger fucking me.

"Yes. Fuck me," I said. "Fuck me." Being so aggressive was unlike me, but I couldn't be anything else with him. He brought the animal out of me and was unleashing my inner beast.

I reached down and took hold of his cock, pulling it, guiding it to my pussy which pulsated in need for more.

Having mercy, Mr. D lowered his full weight on top of me and put his cock at my entrance. Once he was positioned, he paused, looked at my face and lowered his lips to mine. He pressed his tongue past my lips at the exact time that he pushed his dick inside of me.

I gasped and clung to his back as his girth spread me wide. I loved the bite of pain. I wanted more. I wanted to feel him so deep that my body would scream out for reprieve. Harder, faster, I wanted the ultimate claiming from this man.

He did not disappoint me, because that is exactly how he fucked me. He wasn't gentle. This was not lovemaking. He fucked. He fucked good and hard.

In and out, deeper and deeper. It didn't take long before electricity was shooting from my pussy all the way through every nerve ending in my body.

"That's right. Come for me," he demanded as my body tensed and milked his cock in my pleasure.

I mewled his name as sensations exploded from within, but he only kept them going as he drove inside of me at an even and steady pace, summoning another orgasm to surface.

He pulled out just enough to flip me over onto my belly. He then took a handful of hair as he spread my legs wide. He positioned himself between them and took me from behind with a groan and a tug of my hair.

With his free hand, he slapped my ass and said, "This pussy of yours is so fucking tight."

I responded to his carnal praise by pressing my ass into him and meeting each aggressive thrust. My back was arched, my head pulled back, and my mouth open as I cried out while more pleasure rocked my body.

He continued to claim my body until with one final thrust, he came inside of me with a groan that filled the room with his completion.

I had never felt so content and proud of myself before.

I could make a man like Mr. D come in such a way.

It was me.

I did this.

As he relaxed his grip on my hair, and lay on top of me, I knew I had slayed a beast tonight. I had conquered my very own dragon.

Mr. D was mine.

He would be mine beyond just tonight.

As his breathing steadied, he rolled off of me, reached under my arms, and pulled me up to the pillow and adjusted the blankets so they were covering me. Was he tucking me into his bed? For the night?

"Stay with me," I said as I feared he would get up and go to the couch when he didn't settle in next to me.

"We acted without thinking tonight," he said, looking down into my eyes.

"I don't want to think. Why do we always have to think? I'm ready to feel. To feel anything but what

I've been feeling lately. I just want to fall asleep in your arms."

He acted on my words and positioned us so that I rested my head on his chest as his arms held me to him. I could hear the beating of his heart, and I knew that minute that I made the right decision in crawling into bed with him. It was right. Others would argue. But for me, for him, it was right.

"Mr. D?" I asked softly, looking up into his eyes as he pulled the blanket up over my shoulder. "Can we not think of Black Mountain Academy this weekend? Can it just be us? You and me and nothing else. Just for the weekend. Then we can face reality."

His face hardened and I saw such uncertainty in his eyes. "A break from reality sounds like a good idea right now," he said.

11

MR. D

It was a blur. That's the only way to explain the lust-filled... mistake? It was a mistake. A mistake... right? Jesus, I knew better than this. I could shatter my entire life into a million pieces all because of what I just did with a student. A fucking student!

I had never crossed this line before. I hadn't so much as even looked at a student or admired one from afar. Being a man in this profession, I'd always been extremely cautious on how I acted, what I said, and even where my eyes landed. I didn't even allow myself to get involved with teachers or parents of students. I didn't get messy. I stayed squeaky clean.

Until now.

And it wasn't just the having sex part where the line was crossed. Having dinner with her, sitting and watching a movie. We were acting like a couple. Like two people who had reached a point in their relationship where they could just chill and be content. Spending time with Corrine had felt so simple, easy, and frankly... fun. I didn't do shit like this with other women in my life. I was never one to settle. Walls have always guarded my heart, and that's how I liked it. But with Corrine...

Fuck. A huge line was crossed.

Corrine's deep breathing told me she was fast asleep, but I wondered if I would ever be able to rest again. My mind swam in a million directions as I stared up at the ceiling trying to process what I did and how to fix it.

It could never happen again.

But as if Corrine could read my thoughts, she pressed her butt back and up against me, snuggling in close. It felt right. So fucking right. If I wasn't a principal and she the student, I wouldn't be having these thoughts of how wrong tonight was. Because my body was telling me a completely different story. For the first time in my life, my body lit up. It nearly exploded with a need and a hunger that I hadn't felt before. It wasn't just fucking because I had a naked girl in my bed asking for it. It felt as if I had been waiting for this feeling. The pull was so damn strong, that even though warning bells were banging in my head the entire time, I couldn't resist her. There was no way I'd ever be able to say no. Which was the most terrifying thought of all.

I knew I was walking down a dangerous path with Corrine. I knew this wasn't going to end well. How could it? And yet, there was no way I could turn her away. No way I could push her body away from mine as she slept soundly in my bed. There was no way I could resist the temptation of the forbidden. I was going to risk it all, and there wasn't anything my voice of reason could say to talk me out of it.

I'd lose my job over this. Not only would I lose my job, but this would follow me to future employment. I'd forever be the principal who crossed the line and fucked a student. No one would ask or even care that she was of age. No one would assume it was consensual. I'd be a sexual predator forever. Branded.

So why? Why risk it? I knew deep down we're going to get caught eventually. And the reality is that if Corrine and I somehow get through this weekend not getting caught, it would be a miracle. Eyes and ears were all around us, and we were tempting fate by even driving in the same car.

Corrine's body tensed, jerked, and she sat up in a jolt, looking around.

I reached for her and pulled her back to bed, stroking her hair. "It's okay. You're with me. You're safe."

I didn't know why I felt this need to protect her. To care for her. It was powerful, it was all consuming, and it gave me a purpose I didn't realize I was missing. Maybe because she had no one. Maybe because I had no one. Maybe that's why... two people alone who had been seeking comfort. She needed a protector, and I needed someone to protect.

Stop thinking.

Stop thinking.

For now, sleep.

Tomorrow you can think again.

"You're with me," I repeated so she'd lie back down and go to sleep.

Her glassy eyes connected with mine before she closed them again, curved her body to mine, and whispered, "And you're with me."

And with her soft little words, I became undone.

Yes, I was with her. I'd stay that way.

Consequences or not.

12

Corrine

"We really should get up and start the day," he said as he kissed me on the top of the head.

We had spent the entire morning having sex and cuddling. I could have remained like that all day.

"Let's get in the shower," he said.

He bent down and lifted my limp and satisfied body. He didn't seem to find me heavy in the slightest, and I found the new experience of being carried by someone enjoyable. It made me feel safe, protected and nurtured. Like I was a delicate princess... too special to walk. I wrapped my arms around his neck and allowed him to carry me to the bathroom in his cradled embrace. I didn't say anything. Nor did he. I just held.

He placed me outside the shower and turned on the water. Although the water shot out of the shower head at a bitterly cold temperature, splashing on us in tiny droplets, Mr. D quickly adjusted the taps until it was delightfully warm as I entered the stall. The water washed away the remnants of last night and this morning and washed away any signs of what we had just done. Yet, a pleasure in the most taboo of ways remained. We had sex. Mr. D and I had sex... multiple times.

He discarded his boxer briefs and stepped into the shower himself. He was naked. And although I had seen him naked last night, this was the first man I truly had ever seen completely nude in broad daylight.

I stepped to the side a bit so we could both share the streaming water. I wanted to examine every inch of his body with my eyes, with my hands, and even my tongue. Clearly last night, and even this morning, wasn't enough. My appetite for more grew.

"Hand me that bottle," he said, pointing to the shampoo.

I did so, and he squeezed some into his palm and then reached for my hair and began to massage it into my scalp.

I moaned.

I couldn't help it. It felt so good, and the loving act was not lost on me. I never had someone do something so tender and affectionate to me before.

He continued to work the shampoo into my hair as the floral fragrance wafted up my nose, reviving my neglected soul. I actually felt cared for.

"You have gorgeous hair," he said softly. His nude body was so close to mine, yet it did not touch, nor did I feel like the act was his foreplay for more sex. He was simply doing this to be kind.

"I've never had anyone wash my hair before. Well unless you count the hairdresser, but I've never had... this. I'm not used to... attention."

"You deserve this every day," he mumbled, so low that it seemed he hadn't planned for me to actually hear what he said.

He used the rest of the soapy lather on his hands and ran it over my entire body. It wasn't sexual. It wasn't lecherous. It was simply a man cleaning a woman.

"You know we're breaking all the rules. We shouldn't be doing this." His words weren't cruel, but they still stung. I didn't want this to be wrong when I knew it felt right.

I looked at him as he helped me rinse the shampoo out of my hair. "Do you always follow the rules?" I wondered if I was expected to agree, because I didn't want to.

He nodded. "Usually the big ones. Yes. This is a pretty fucking massive rule we are ignoring."

"Why? I'm nineteen."

"Because you're a student of Black Mountain Academy. I'm the principal... at least until someone catches wind of this."

"I would never tell anyone."

"It's not just that." He leaned down and softly kissed my lips. "We both know this isn't going to end well."

"Why?" I said as I lowered my hand to his dick, loving that it instantly twitched and hardened. "You think I can't keep up with you?" I licked my lips and considered dropping to my knees to show him just how wrong he was about us. We could work. We could *make* it work.

"We are both at very different stages of our lives."

"I believe you're overthinking," I said, not wanting to ruin this perfect moment. "Let's just live in the moment. Right now." I gave a wicked smile as I stroked his dick. "We already crossed the line. We might as well enjoy this side of forbidden."

Mr. D swallowed hard but didn't respond.

I didn't mind the touch of bad. I actually enjoyed the smell of possible destruction. At least it made me feel something, anything. I wasn't numb. I had felt nothing for so long that even feeling dirty and soiled by temptations was better than the void of nothing I had been spinning in for so long.

He didn't argue with me. Instead, he reached for my chin, pushed me down to my knees, and pulled my face to the tip of his hardened flesh. He continued to hold my chin as he pressed past my lips. I didn't have a choice but to open wide as the thickness of his member filled every inch of open space in my mouth. The weight was heavy against my tongue, and as he pressed deeper inside, I struggled not to gag as his full size touched the back of my throat. He released my chin and placed both of his hands on each side of my head, and gently began rocking his hips. The friction of my lips along his smooth and velvety skin caused his penis to twitch and grow even bigger.

I looked up at him, and for the first time since we entered the shower, he wasn't staring at me. Instead, he had his eyes closed, his head tilted back slightly, and my pussy pulsated knowing I was giving him pleasure by having my mouth around him.

Tasting the saltiness, smelling the musky odor, and feeling the black hairs that circled his sex brush up against my face each time he drove as far into my mouth as he could, lit my body on fire even as the water from the shower extinguished the flames. I held my position, kept my mouth open, and tried to give this man the best blowjob of his life. I think it helped that he kept his hands firmly placed on my head. It offered me the support and guidance that I so desperately needed. He chose the pace and set the depth of how far he would fuck my mouth. I was his vessel to fuck and I loved every second of it.

I would worship this cock as I knew he wanted me to do.

In and out he went, plundering my mouth. I watched his face tighten, heard his breathing increase, and felt his thrusts grow in aggression.

A deep moan came from the depths of his belly and exited his lips on a growl. Hot liquid shot from his cock and coated the back of my throat, forcing me to swallow the salty, milky matter. He released my head from his grip, and with a gentle touch of his fingertip, he swiped at the remnants of his release that seeped from the corner of my mouth.

He pulled me back to standing and continued to bathe the rest of my body and then did the same to his. Silently turning off the water, he reached for two towels and handed one to me. Once he dried his body off, he used his towel to help dry my hair. He gently squeezed the water out, massaging my scalp again. Closing my eyes, I just allowed the feelings of good to wash over me.

"What should we do today?" he asked as he reached for my hand and pulled me out of the bathroom. "It's going to be a nice day, and I don't know about you, but I could use a day out in nature. Something that allows some fresh air."

"What do you have in mind?"

"Kayaking sounds good," he answered simply as he sat me down on the bed. "Ever been?"

He walked over to a dresser and pulled out a shirt and pair of shorts. I clung to the towel around my body as goosebumps covered my flesh.

"No," I answered. I wasn't really the outdoorsy type. "I don't really get along with Mother Nature."

"It's easy, and you'll love it," he said, leaning in and kissing me on the cheek. "You just haven't been introduced to her properly yet by the right person."

"And you are that person?" My belly flipped and my skin sizzled. He was acting like we were going on a... on a date.

"Get ready and we'll go get breakfast on the way to the lake."

13

MR. D

It had only been a couple of days, and we were moving at warp speed. Sex, cuddling, waking up together in the morning, showering, having breakfast together, and now spending the day with each other like an official date was not the way I liked to live my life. I hadn't had a relationship in years, and frankly, I preferred it that way. Casual sex kept things simple, and I liked simple.

But Corrine was anything but simple.

I shouldn't have had sex with her, but at the same time, I wasn't going to live my life with regrets. And I didn't regret having sex with Corrine and acting so fast and furious. Maybe if I were a wiser man, I would. Maybe I should be promising it would never happen again, but that wasn't what I wanted. I did want her, again, and again, and again.

Was I some sex-crazed creep who just wanted young, tight pussy? I'm sure many would view me as that if they knew what happened last night, and then this morning, and hopefully multiple more times this weekend. But I didn't care. It was nobody's business what we did. Just ours, and as long as we could keep it that way, we would be able to create our own version of *simple*.

"You make it look so easy," she said, paddling my second kayak that, until today, had yet to be used. I never did understand why I had bought two kayaks, but it seemed like the right thing to do. Now I was doing the couple thing... odd, but I liked it.

"You'll get the hang of it," I said. "It's not like a canoe where you have to worry about tipping over."

"I feel like I could," she said, looking at the crystal-clear water of Devil's Bluff Lake. "And it looks freezing."

"Even strokes," I coached as I positioned my kayak next to hers and matched her pace.

"I actually really like this," she said. "It's pretty here. I've never been."

I found that to be shocking. "You live in Black Mountain but have never been to Devil's Bluff Lake. This is a landmark. How is that?"

"You've never met my mother. We didn't do nature." She paddled in silence for a few moments. "We didn't do much."

"You traveled a lot together, right? So, you must have done some things."

She huffed. "I traveled with a nanny and her team of staff. I maybe saw her an hour a day. Maybe. And she was notorious for arriving someplace, meeting up with old friends or lovers and disappearing for days. Her staff knew they just needed to watch over me, and she would someday return."

"Sounds lonely," I said.

"I don't know what it feels like to *not* feel alone."

"Well, you aren't alone anymore. I'm here to help you get through all this."

She stopped paddling as we reached the middle of the lake and then looked at me. "Am I a burden to you, Mr. D?"

The way her eyes looked as she asked the question, I instantly regretted being in the kayaks and separate. I wanted to hold her, stroke her hair and give her loving kisses of affection. This poor girl. She needed love. It was so obvious to see, and my heart longed to be the man to give it.

"First of all, you are far from a burden. Second, I think you can stop calling me Mr. D when we aren't in school."

"I like Mr. D," she said with a giggle. "It's catchy." She looked around at the trees, the huge rock structure known as Devil's Tooth and took a deep breath. "I didn't even know what your real name was until I heard that woman in your room call you Drew. But it doesn't suit you. I think you'll always be Mr. D to me."

"How about we just keep it D then? Cut the mister part."

She nodded. "D." With a big smile, she said. "I like that... D."

"And, Corrine, you will never be a burden to me. You never need to feel that way. It saddens me to think you were brought up to think that way."

"I know I threw myself on you."

"You couldn't control the situation that brought us together. And who cares at this point? If you haven't noticed, I like you."

"Because we had sex?" she asked with narrowed eyes as she nibbled her lip.

I chuckled. "As great as our sex was, there's more to us than that. I've had lots of sex with women I don't really care for. It's easy, no hassle, and just the way I am usually. But you're refreshing. I actually like spending time with you outside of the bedroom."

She smiled and the tops of her cheeks pinkened. "Do you have a lot of women in your life?"

"I'm far from a playboy if that's what you're asking. I tend to keep to myself. But are there women..." I laughed. "I think you saw for yourself."

"Shelly right?"

"Yeah, Shelly. And before you ask, no, there's nothing between us. Maybe she would like there to be, but she's not my type."

"What is your type?"

"Clearly I like damsels in distress."

"Does my age bother you?"

I really liked how straightforward and to the point this woman was. She said what she thought, and I appreciated her boldness. If she thought it, she asked it.

"Not your age... not really. I would rather you not be a student at Black Mountain Academy. It weirds me out. It's risky as hell. But I also know that had we met at a bar or something—" *She wasn't even twenty-one. Idiot.* "Well, if we met under different circumstances, I'm not sure I wouldn't pursue you simply because of age. What about you? Does my age bother you?"

"I find maturity sexy," she said. "The men I've been interested in in the past tended to be older too. Have you met the boys at Black Mountain Academy? I would rather stay clear of them. I'm not saying I'm more mature—"

"But you are," I interrupted. "You most certainly are more worldly. Hell, you are more traveled and experienced with real adventure than I am."

"If you call being holed up as a near orphan in every five-star hotel in the world as adventure, then yes, I got that on you."

"I find you fascinating, Corrine. I can tell I've only scratched the surface when it comes to you."

She shrugged. "I suppose so. But I'm sure there's a lot I don't know about you as well."

"Well, I for one am looking forward to learning more. And we have a great weekend ahead of us. Tomorrow, I was thinking we could go on this hike I've been hearing about. It's near Angel's Sin which is a smaller lake fed from this one we are in."

She rolled her eyes and playfully sighed. "You're going to turn me into one of those tree-hugging Patagonia yuppies, aren't you?"

I reached my hand into the water and splashed her. "Come on, let's keep going."

14

Mr. D

I had never hated a Monday more than I did today.

"Can't we call in sick?" Corrine whined as she cuddled her naked body against mine. "Pretty please?"

Kissing the top of her head and trying to ignore my hardening cock, I said, "Someone has missed too many days of school, or we would."

"I could write a really good excuse. Get a pass." She ran her palm along my chest, making small circles down to my cock.

I took hold of her hand and brought it to my lips and kissed it. "Someone in this bed needs to graduate."

"Mr. Deeeeeeee..." she whined and then pouted her lips.

I didn't blame her one bit for the pout because it was definitely how I was feeling as well. We'd had an amazing weekend. Spending time with Corrine filled me with a happiness and a level of contentment I hadn't felt in a very long time. We were doing all the activities I loved, but it was fun seeing them for the first time through her eyes. She had lived such a sheltered life from all the normal things in a day-to-day existence, and I loved being the one to introduce them to her. I wished the weekend didn't have to come to an end.

Corrine snuggled more deeply into my arms. I hadn't let her out of my sight all weekend and doing so today was going to suck.

"We should get breakfast going before we're late," I suggested, trying to force both of us out of bed.

The truth was that I liked her right there in my arms. Her body warm, melting as I thought of all the sex we had shared over such a short but passion-filled weekend. Lots of slow, lingering kisses, mixed with passionate gasps and pleas for more. The woman drove me insane with her touches. I was far from inexperienced, but this girl knew how to light up my body like no one else.

"I'm not hungry," she said. "Let's just stay here."

"I thought for sure we worked up an appetite. Is it time for another round?" I suggested. "A quickie before our showers?"

She laughed. "I'm not sure I can. I think you've truly worn me out."

"Then breakfast it is."

She raised her head to look at me. "You really are going to make us both go to school aren't you."

"You better listen to the principal... or else."

"Yes, sir. Whatever you say, sir."

"Exactly," I said and chuckled.

She sighed and collapsed against my chest once more. "I don't want to face reality."

"We have no choice. Playtime is over. Responsibility is calling." I freed myself from her embrace and stood naked at the side of the bed. "Don't make me have to discipline you like the naughty girl you are."

Corrine laughed. "Promises, promises."

I bent down and kissed the tip of her nose. "Promise me you won't move. I have something I want to give you."

She rolled onto her stomach, propped herself up on her arms, and smiled up at me. "Trying to bribe me so I'll go to school and be a good girl?"

"Got to do what I got to do all in the name of education." I smiled. "Stay right there. I'll be right back."

I kissed her in that slow, sweet way that always made her release a tiny mewl.

I came back in an instant with a simply wrapped gift in my hands.

I sat it on the bed in front of her. "Open it."

She looked at the box with surprise. Looking up to my face, she searched my eyes for some hint as to what was inside.

"Open it," I urged.

She slowly removed the wrapping paper. She lifted the lid and smiled. "What's this?"

"You'll see."

She dug through the tissue paper, finally finding a silver key. She gasped. "Is this a key to…"

I pressed a fingertip to her lips. "To my place. I want you to feel like you can always come here whenever you want. I don't want you to ever be afraid. And if your house makes you scared, then I want you to always feel you have a safe haven to run to. Whether I'm here or not, this is now your safe place."

She held the key in her palm and stared with tears in her eyes. She nodded. "Are you sure?"

"It's important for me to know you are safe. It's also just as important for me to know you *feel* that way. So, yes. I'm sure."

She tugged me down onto the bed. Forgetting about our time limit and being late for school, she kissed me with the same passion that exploded from within my heart.

Corrine looked back down at the key and held it to her chest. "You've made me feel like the most special woman in the world."

I kissed her hand. "You are. And it's long overdue for someone to make you feel that way."

I reached for her, dragging her nude body into my arms, holding her with all my strength. She raised her face, waiting as I lowered my head, my lips coming down on hers for a long, ravenous kiss. A kiss that made time stop. She cuddled into my arms, taking a deep breath of my scent.

But it was time to face the outside.

"Shower time," I said, reaching around and swatting her ass.

"Fine," she said as she put her hands on her hips, "but only if you promise to make me those tamales you raved about tonight."

I watched her walk to the bathroom completely naked, her brown hair cascading down her back. "It's a date," I called after her.

She looked over her shoulder at me and winked. "Care to join me?"

Fuck yes, I wanted to join her, but I also knew that if I did, we would be late. We still had to swing by the mechanic's on the way to school because they had called and told her that her car was ready. Her having her own vehicle would make things easier. We didn't risk being seen driving together, and we had already made room in the garage so she could pull in and keep her car concealed.

"Come on, hurry up," I ordered, feeling excited to start the day only so I could end it with her.

But the day most definitely became your classic Monday. I had no idea how awful and long the day would be now that I had a taste of actual fun with Corrine. It seemed like one thing happened after another, students were acting up all over the place, and the drama was high in every corner of every hallway. To top it off, I had to confront Shelly and officially call off whatever it was that we had. I couldn't risk any more surprise visits now that Corrine was staying with me, and though Shelly took it well, it sucked, and I wasn't even entirely convinced she was taking me seriously.

It had been one hell of a day, and just as I was getting ready to start packing up, I decided to try calling Corrine's mother again. We needed to do something. As much as I enjoyed having Corrine in my life, and even in my bed, I knew that we needed to address the stalker issue eventually. We couldn't keep sneaking around with her living at my place. We were bound to be discovered... and yet, I didn't want it to end either. But I did want her safe, and that would be my first priority.

But in addition to wanting Corrine safe, I wanted her fucking mother to give a damn about her wellbeing. Yes, I felt that Corrine and I had reached a level in our... *relationship* that I could help her vet some security guards and make sure we got the right person in place. I also could help her with updating her alarm system and adding cameras.

I could also keep a closer eye on that Kevin kid, because there was a high chance that this was just a matter of a pimple-faced boy having a crush and no balls to express it. I could be there for Corrine, and I planned to, but I also knew she needed her mother. She needed to know that someone out there loved her and would be by her side no matter what. She needed her god damn mother.

I was actually surprised when someone picked up the phone. So much so, that I wasn't quite ready to speak.

"Hello?" The voice sounded jovial, loud, excited. There was some kind of party going on in the background.

"May I speak with Candy Parker?"

"Speaking."

"Ms. Parker?" The loud music in the background made it very difficult to hear, and I could only imagine how hard it was for her to hear me.

"Hello?" She giggled and yelled at someone to lower the music.

"Ms. Parker," I said again. "This is Mr. Dawson, the school principal at Black Mountain Academy. I've been trying to get hold of you for days."

"Oh, sorry. We've been at sea, island-hopping. I sometimes get a signal on this yacht, and sometimes not." The music lowered but was still loud enough that I was growing frustrated. "Who did you say you were again?"

"I'm the principal of your daughter's school."

"Where?"

"Black Mountain Academy," I shouted, partly due to the loud music, but also because I wanted to jump through the phone and strangle the woman.

"Are you talking about Corrine?"

Who the hell else would I be talking about?

"Black Mountain Academy? When did she start going there?"

Was she drunk? High? Why was this conversation so fucking difficult?

"Ms. Parker, you would have had to sign papers for your daughter to attend the school. The tuition had to be paid. Uniform costs? Were you not aware that your daughter has been attending this school?"

"Corrine is free to do what she chooses. If she wants to go to Black Mountain School—"

"Academy," I interrupted.

"Yeah, whatever. I'm fine with it. Is that why you're calling? To ask my permission or something?"

"No. I was originally calling because your daughter has been missing a lot of school. So much so, that her chances of graduating have been put in jeopardy."

"Sounds like Corrine," she said. "I don't know what you expect me to do about it. She's an adult now. She can make her own choices." She giggled again, and I could faintly hear another man speaking nearby. "I'm on the phone, but I'll be there in a sec."

"Ms. Parker—"

"I didn't even know she was in Black Mountain. I haven't seen or spoken to her for—" She giggled again. "Give me a second," she whispered off the phone to someone else.

Closing my eyes and taking a deep breath, I continued, "There's a much larger issue that has come up in all this. To make a long story short..." especially since I could hear people partying on the other end, and I figured Candy Parker was already losing interest in this phone call, "your daughter is in danger."

"What?"

I wasn't sure if she was asking the question because she couldn't hear me, or because she didn't believe me, or maybe because it seemed so unlikely.

"I said your daughter's in danger." My voice raised even more. "She has a stalker who's been harassing her for quite some time."

She remained silent for a few moments, and the music faded as if she'd moved to another area of the yacht. "I'm sorry, what was your name again?"

"Drew Dawson."

"Mr. Dawson, I don't believe my daughter has a stalker, and she most definitely is not in danger."

"Excuse me?" Her words were like a punch to the gut. What kind of mother would instantly doubt this? I expected some level of concern.

"There are things about my daughter you may not know about. Corrine is a compulsive liar among other things. This is just what she does."

I clenched my jaw so tightly that I had to actually concentrate on relaxing it enough so I could speak. "She's not making this up. I've seen it for myself."

"Seen the stalker?"

"No, but I saw what the stalker was doing to her with my own eyes."

"I know my daughter, and—"

"Ms. Parker, I wouldn't be concerned and calling you if I had any doubt," I cut in. "Your daughter's in danger and needs more security. I don't know where you are, but she really could use you right now."

"Where is she now?" she asked flatly. "Is she still at our vacation house?"

It was time to jump off the cliff and hope my confession didn't cause me to fall to my death. "She's with me. We called the police, and they agreed she wasn't safe at her house. Since she didn't have anyone else to stay with, and since I was with her—"

"She's staying with *you*?" She didn't sound angry, but rather it sounded like more of a statement than a question.

I heard her release a deep sigh, but her response confused me. I had expected her to be alarmed, angry, even skeptical as to why a grown man my age would be concerning himself with someone of Corrine's age. I had expected her to question my judgment, as well as my morals and professionalism. I even expected her to demand my head on a platter and want me fired.

I got none of that.

"It was a temporary solution until we could get hold of you. I didn't anticipate it taking a couple of days."

"Mr. Dawson, I'm not worried about my daughter." There was a long pause. "I'm worried about you."

Me?

"I don't understand what—"

"This isn't the first time Corrine has done this," she interrupted.

"Done what?"

"This is a cry for attention."

"Ms. Parker, with all due respect—"

"Has she told you she was committed for a time? In a mental hospital," Candy blurted. "I'm sure it's not mentioned in her records since we worked hard to keep those sealed, and I doubt she actually told anyone. But she was. About a year ago. Why do you think she is having to repeat her senior year?"

"Committed? For what?"

"For stalking, Mr. Dawson. She had a very unhealthy obsession. *She* was the stalker. Not the other way around."

My ears rang, and my breath came out in short puffs of air. I stared down at Corrine's file and tried to focus on the letters of her name in order to stay in the present.

There had to be some sort of mistake.

"I understand your concern, Mr. Dawson, but I can assure you that this story she told you is all made up. This is all part of her plan."

Plan? What plan?

"Oh, and Mr. Dawson. I would be careful if I were you. The man she tormented and nearly destroyed his life was a teacher from her old school," Candy added. "It sounds like you're her next prey."

15

When I got a text from D asking me to come to his office *NOW*, I knew something was wrong. Maybe he had gotten hold of my mother and realized just how much of a flake she truly was. Maybe he'd had to deal with Bill which would put anyone in a foul mood. Or maybe I was reading into his text and he wasn't in a bad mood at all. Maybe he just wanted to see me because he missed me. Maybe it was friendly mid-day flirting.

As I entered his office, I could tell there was nothing friendly about this meeting. He stood on the other side of his desk with his arms crossed, his jaw firm and his eyebrows angled down.

"I got your text," I began, not really sure what to say.

"Sit," he ordered.

I did so, not sure what I should ready myself for.

"I just got off the phone with your mother."

I raised my head and my heart skipped. "Is she coming home?" Maybe she would take Mr. D calling as to mean this situation was serious, and she would actually come home to help deal with it.

"Why would she come home?" he said, sitting down in his seat, never taking his eyes off of me. "That would mean that there was something she could actually come back to address. She told me she had given up on helping you a long time ago."

His words hurt. Of course she would say something like that. I didn't know why I expected anything more. But it hurt more hearing her thoughts come from D in such a harsh way.

"I don't understand why you're talking this way," I began.

"You need to tell me the fucking truth. Now!" I had never seen D so angry before. If we weren't sitting in his office, I would actually be more afraid. He appeared as if he were going to actually erupt.

"That's just my mother. She never believes me," I said, hating that my voice quivered so much as I spoke.

"Were you committed to a mental hospital for stalking?"

And there it was.

A blow to my face, to the torso, to my very soul.

D didn't have to actually punch me for me to feel as if I had just been beaten to a pulp.

"Answer me," he said in an even tone, but his face told me all I needed to know.

My mother had revealed everything. I hadn't thought she would ever speak of it to anyone due to her overwhelming shame and how hard she tried to keep it hidden.

"It's not what you think..."

I had no idea how to defend this. I had no idea what to say or do. Should I just run out of the office and never look back. Should I deny it all? Should I… should I… I had no idea what to do.

"I'm done playing these fucked up games with you, Corrine. It's time you tell me the fucking truth. I'm not going to keep asking you."

His warning was most definitely a threat.

"Yes," I said. "For a short time. A couple of months to get my head on straight. I was just going through a lot and—"

"Did you stalk a teacher at your old school."

"What did my mother tell you?" I asked.

"It doesn't matter what your mother told me. What I care about is what you tell me. I deserve the truth. So, I'm going to ask you again. Did you stalk a teacher from your old school?"

Stalk was such a strong word.

Did I hide in shadows outside his house?

Did I watch his every move?

Did I fantasize what it would be like to be with him?

Did I obsess over every little thing he did?

Did I manipulate situations so we could be together?

Did I stalk my old teacher?

"Yes," I said.

D inhaled deeply, sucking all the breathable air from the room, and I nearly suffocated on what was left.

"But I got help for that. I realized that all I had for that man was an infatuation. Nothing more. Nothing like what you and I have," I said.

D let out a laugh that sounded anything but jovial. "What *we* have? What we have?" He took another deep breath before asking, "Have you been stalking me, Corrine?"

I shook my head vigorously. "No, it's not like that. I know how this might look, but—"

"Was there anyone really stalking you? Did you make it all up?" He ran his fingers through his hair. "Fuck... was this some sort of play for attention? For *my* attention? Is this what you did to your teacher before?"

"D... I..."

"Stop!" he snapped. "You'll call me Mr. D from now on. Having you call me anything else was a mistake. I'm your principal, and I expect the formal respect."

I swallowed back the pain of his words. "Mr. D," I corrected. "I know this looks really bad, and I understand why you're upset—"

"Was there a stalker?" His voice raised an octave, but he still kept his outer shell cool and collected. Once again, I was happy we were in his office at school, because if we were in private, I don't think he would have been half as calm as he was appearing to be.

Was there a stalker?

Was there a stalker?

Was there a stalker?

The truth would be a dagger to what D and I had created. Any chance of anything more would be over.

Lie or tell the truth?

Deceive or be honest?

"Corrine!" he said in a near hiss. "Was this some fucked up game? Was there ever a stalker?"

"Yes!" I blurted. "Yes, there was a stalker."

He seemed to visibly relax at my words until I continued on.

"I was the stalker. It was me. It's always been me." The confession burned my tongue.

D pushed away from the desk as if we were too close. All color drained from his face and his eyes closed, then opened, then closed again.

Let the confession begin.

"When I started at Black Mountain Academy, I knew I had to have you in my life. It wasn't just your appearance but the way you dominated a room when you entered. I watched you from afar, and I knew. I felt it deep down in my gut that you were the man for me. And yes, I know it sounds crazy, but I just knew." I had to pause to suck in oxygen as I'd been holding my breath as I spoke. "I also knew that my old behavior I had worked so hard to break was coming back. The doors were my warning. I knew I was falling back into the obsessive and dark rabbit hole again, and you were the prey of my upcoming hunt. I knew this... but I couldn't stop."

"Jesus, Corrine, I need you to leave my office now."

"Wait," I shot out. "So, yes, it started out all the same as before, but something happened. *You* happened. I didn't have to stalk you, because you were there for me. I didn't have to watch your every move from afar because you remained by my side. You didn't make me have to lie or manipulate you because you accepted me for me. You made me feel safe, protected, and cared for. All the dark shadows that were threatening to consume me like they were doing before were disappearing. The more I was with you, the more normal I felt."

"No, this is not normal. This is fucked up." He crossed his arms over his chest and his eyes narrowed. "You did lie. You did manipulate."

"At first," I agreed with a little nod, feeling the tears burn the back of my eyes. "But I swear to you, it all changed. My 'game' and my 'plan' changed when I realized I didn't need them."

He remained silent. Staring at me with disbelief written all over his face.

"I know how this looks," I said. "I'm not crazy... well, not in a way that you have to be afraid of me or anything. Even if you ask the teacher in L.A., he would tell you that he didn't press charges or anything. I didn't harm him." My voice lowered as I looked down at my hands. "My therapist told me that this was my way of coping with my lack of love and affection growing up. That I don't believe that I have the ability to find love in a healthy way because I've never experienced it before."

"I don't give a fuck why or what some asshole doctor says. I care about what you did. And I don't even know exactly what you did." He paused, rubbed his jaw a few times and then asked, "So you had no stalker? Right?"

"I never had one physically. But mentally... the voices stalked me. Until you."

"So, what about the doors? I saw them open with my own eyes."

"That first night, I ran upstairs to close the doors, but painted WHORE on my wall while you were checking and closing the doors downstairs. I then sent a text to my handyman who had been doing some work on the house to come in set some mice traps. I asked him to open all the doors for me. He did so while we were at dinner."

The confession made me sick to my stomach. Here I was trying to convince D... Mr. D... that I wasn't crazy, but hearing the words made me sound pretty damn insane.

"Why?" he asked.

"Because I knew the type of man you were. And that if you felt my life was in danger, you wouldn't leave me. You would either stay with me—which is what I had originally thought would happen—or at the very least care about me. I would get on your radar more than just as a student."

"And the police? Why call them all the times before if there was never a stalker?"

I shrugged. "Attention." I swallowed back the shakiness in my throat. "When my mind began to spin, and I felt like the walls were closing in, I would call them to distract me."

"And being late to school? Was your story about closing the doors obsessively made up as well?"

"That's true," I said. "I do it when I feel like I'm losing control. It's my way to try to keep my inner demons away." I licked my dry lips, wishing for a glass of water. "But it's what made me start falling for you. Every time I would go into the office to get a note, I would see you. I would watch you. And I knew... we were soulmates."

"Don't fucking say that," he bit, slamming his palm on the desk. He quickly looked over my shoulder to see if he was too loud and if any of the faculty had heard him. "Do you realize what you did? I risked my career for you. I went against everything that was right to be wrong for you. For you! Do you understand that? Do you get that you fucked with my life?"

"That wasn't my intent. I never wanted to get you into any trouble."

"No? What was your plan then? To make me fall in love with you so we could live happily ever after?"

"Would that have been so bad?" I asked softly.

"You are fucking insane," he said, pure venom shooting from his eyes. "I want you out of my office immediately. I also want you to stay the fuck away from me. Do. We. Understand?"

"Please don't say this. I understand you're angry. I get that—"

"Angry can't even begin to describe what I feel."

"We had something... You can't deny that."

"What we had was some twisted schoolgirl obsession. You need help, Corrine, but I'm done offering it."

"Please—"

"Go back to L.A. and finish out the school year. I could push for you to be committed again, and maybe I should. But I'm giving you the opportunity to leave. Leave." He pointed at the door. "I mean it. Don't you dare stalk me, come near me, or even think of me again."

I stood up, tears no longer being held back, and walked to the door. Did I really expect for him to not react the way he was?

I looked over my shoulder and said, "I fell in love with you. And it wasn't the madness that did. It was my genuine and clear-thinking heart."

Without saying another word, I exited his office... and closed the door.

16

_____

Was it possible to feel betrayed when you were the one guilty of betraying?

Why would my mother tell the principal of my new school about my past? It was my dirty, dirty secret, and she knew it. Hell, she had hired some fancy PR company to try to bury the info so deep that the media would never discover the fact that I went away to "mental rehab" as my mother put it. She wanted it swept under the rug more than I did.

So why in the world would she out me to someone she didn't know?

I hadn't anticipated that at all, or I would have never given D all the tools I had in order to try to reach her.

I wanted to choke on my own spit.

I wanted to collapse against the lockers and never walk again.

I wanted to—

"Corrine!" I heard called from behind me. I quickly swiped the tears away from my eyes and saw Kevin running down the hall toward me. "Wait up."

He was the last person I wanted to speak to right now, and frankly, I feared I would vomit or have a nervous breakdown right in front of the Spanish class door. I needed air. I needed to get out of this school as fast as possible.

"Corrine," Kevin said a little winded. "I've been looking for you all day. I've also been texting and calling all weekend. What the fuck is going on?"

I glanced around to make sure no one was paying attention to us—which they weren't of course because beautiful people focused on other beautiful people only—but I wanted to be sure I wasn't part of a scene, and Kevin had a loud voice.

"I'm just going through some stuff right now," I said, lowering my voice so only he could hear.

"Yeah... well, I think this *stuff* you are going through is what we need to talk about."

I tilted my head trying to read him. What was he talking about?

"You've been acting more distant than normal. Off. Every time I go by your house, you aren't there, which is also odd since I'm the only person in this town you really know. So, I hid outside your house Friday as I saw cops leave. I then saw you leave, and I saw who you were with. I also saw him grab and hold your hand."

I froze, knowing what he would say next.

"Are you fucking Mr. D?" He asked the question in a low voice, leaning in as close as he could to me without actually touching.

I didn't want to lie to Kevin. Especially since I was just called out on the ultimate lie and was still reeling from it. But I sure as hell didn't want to tell him the truth either.

And it wasn't like I would ever be able to fuck Mr. D again.

Not now.

Not ever.

I gave a small laugh, realizing it sounded fake the minute I did it. "Have you lost your mind?"

Kevin didn't even flinch. "No, but I'm worried you have. Again." He placed his hand on my upper arm. "This is why you left L.A. To get away from... *that*."

"This isn't like L.A.," I said.

"Really? Because it sure looks like it is. Mr. D? Out of everyone, you choose the principal?"

I couldn't stand there and have this conversation any longer. My knees threatened to buckle, and the voices were whispering in my head.

"I can't talk about this right now."

"You need help, Corrine. I gave you the benefit of the doubt in L.A. I stood by you, shrugged off all the awful rumors, and tried to understand why you were into Mr. Harrison, but now Mr. D. This is fucked up, girl. Totally fucked. This isn't you. I know you, and I know you're spiraling. We need to get you on meds or something."

"Don't pretend to know me," I hissed, wanting to hold my ears so the voices would stop chanting that the doors in the hallways were open. All the doors were open.

Why wouldn't anyone close a fucking door?

"I do know you. I know why you do this. I see you. Call it Daddy issues, call it attention seeking, obsessive behavior—"

"Or just call it a girl looking for love," I said between clenched teeth. "Why does it have to be a mental thing? Why are my feelings wrong? Why does it make me sick in the head? Huh? Answer me that fucking question. Am I not entitled to find love without pills being pushed in my direction?"

"You call this love? He's the principal! The last guy you were into was a teacher! This isn't normal, Corrine. I know you agree with me at least deep down."

"Why does age matter? Maybe I don't want to fuck inexperienced little boys," I snapped.

He reached for my hand, but I pulled it away harshly.

"Corrine," he said calmly as if he were trying to soothe a rabid dog. "I'm your friend. Let me help you."

"I don't need help. I need people to understand me."

"I do. I'm like you. I get it. I know what it's like growing up with no parents to love you. I know what it feels like to be alone. I get you whether you want to admit that or not. But I also know that you can't repeat what happened with Mr. Harrison."

"Stop saying his name," I nearly growled. "I know I fucked that all up. I know I lost it. Okay? I know. But that's not what this is."

"Really? Because it sure looks like it to me. Are you telling me that you and Mr. D fell in love like two star-struck lovers? Or are you going to admit that you hunted his ass from the depths of your fucked up mind just like you did with Mr. Harrison?"

"I told you to stop saying his name." I held my hands to my ears, but the voices only got louder.

And louder.

And even louder.

"You're going to take Mr. D down that black rabbit hole with you," he said.

"Don't worry," I said with a tilted grin. "He jumped out."

I turned on my heels and headed out of the school.

"Corrine!" he called out.

"I'm leaving," I yelled over my shoulder.

And I was.

Mr. D wanted me out of Black Mountain, and it was the least I could do.

I would ignore the voices that told me to sit in my car and watch him from a distance.

I would not be that girl.

I would not obsess.

I would not watch.

I would not wait.

I would not stalk.

I would prove them all wrong. I wasn't crazy. I wasn't crazy. I wasn't crazy.

I would not stalk. I would not stalk...

Fuck that.

Yes, I would.

And he would be going home soon. I would wait. I would wait. I would make it all better.

Yes, the voices were quiet now. They were content with my decision.

Mr. D.

I needed Mr. D.

17

Corrine

Day One:

I will see him. I will make it right.

"Please let me in. I need to explain."

"You need to get off my property right now, Corrine. I've seen you out there in your car. It's sick." Rage danced in the darkness of his eyes, but I couldn't be afraid.

"I fucked up. I know this. But I can explain some of it. Please let me try."

He moved out of the doorway, and I took my chance and entered. I very well could have been entering the den of the beast that would devour me and tear my flesh to shreds, but I didn't want to give up.

As I turned around to face the man I planned to get down on my knees and beg for forgiveness if I had to, I was surprised when he took a handful of my hair and forced his lips onto mine.

The kiss was hard, passionate, aggressive and yet welcomed. He continued to master my mouth with his as he pressed me hard against the wall, causing the paintings hanging nearby to rattle. His actions were far from gentle, but I knew they matched the fury inside that had to be eating him up.

"Take off your fucking clothes," he commanded.

He took a step away and began doing the same.

I brought my shaky fingers to the button of my pants and began doing exactly as he said. If this was my penance to earn his forgiveness, then so be it.

Anything.

I would have done anything.

He pressed his mouth to mine, thrusting his tongue past my lips. I waited for him to bite, to shove, to hurt in order to contrast against such an intimate touch.

I returned the kiss, cautious at first, but did not resist at all.

He grabbed my breast and broke away from the kiss so he could watch my expression. Pinching my nipple hard, I wondered if he waited for a cry, a scream, something. I simply stared as his pupils dilated and his mouth opened slightly in an almost snarl.

Not saying a word, he lowered his hand and pressed his finger into my pussy without any warning at all. My wetness made the invasion smooth and painless, and when I spread my legs wider and moaned in response, I knew I was losing my fucking mind—or what was left to lose. He made me feel that way.

All I wanted was him to hurt me.

Abuse me.

Make it right.

Make all I did go away.

Punish me.

Make me pay.

Thrusting his finger up inside me as deeply as he could, he growled, "Did you think I was a good guy? A nice man who would be easily tricked?" He thrust again, and then again. Each thrust harder than the last. My juices seeped around his finger, coating his palm.

I moaned loudly with each aggressive movement of his hand, clinging to his back as if holding on to life. I was submerged into complete darkness and he was my only beacon of light.

With his other hand, he grabbed my throat and began to squeeze. "I could hurt you right now. I could do things to you that would damage you forever. I could fuck with your mind in ways that you would never recover."

My eyes widened, but I was not afraid. Maybe because I was curious just how he would do that.

Maybe I wanted it.

Maybe I wanted to be taken right to that edge.

My pussy tightened around his finger, and I knew that if he continued, I would come. I was going to come from his threats alone.

In a moment of rage, he flipped me around to face the wall.

I didn't cry. I didn't whimper.

He slapped my ass hard, causing a need to moan and plead for more.

Taking hold of my hair, yanking hard at the scalp, he swatted my ass fiercely again, and then again.

Yes, Mr. D.

Punish me.

I've been bad.

So very very bad.

Breaths of air released from my open mouth, but still no cries for mercy followed. No shouts. No begging to God.

I liked it.

I fucking loved it.

He continued to spank my ass, the sting of his touch burning all the way down to the wet lips of my sex. I would win this battle with him. I knew he wanted me to hate him. I knew he wanted me to fear him. I knew he thought he wanted me to leave his home vowing never to come back. But that wouldn't happen.

It would never happen.

Mr. D would reveal his desire to be with me by the time this night was over.

After spanking my ass several times, aggressively and hard—practically growling with every breath —he shoved me down to the ground, towering over me. "Look at me," he shouted. "You want to play in an adult world, little girl? You want to fuck with people? You want to mess with the minds of others? Well, you picked the wrong fucking person to do it with."

I stared up at him... waiting. I saw pain in his eyes, a deep despair. I saw fury and rage—which I knew would pass. But I did not see hatred. Mr. D did not hate me, and I knew that.

"Answer me," he demanded. "Do you think you can mess with grown ass men and not think there would be consequences?"

"I want the consequences."

"Jesus, you're insane."

"Yes," I answered, my eyes never leaving his. "I am who I am, and I'm not going to deny it."

"You hid this side of you. You lied. You deceived. Shame on me for falling for it," he said between clenched teeth. "But I see you, Corrine. I see clearly now. Never again will I fall for your traps."

Mr. D

Her tiny naked frame lay crumpled on the floor, still pressed up against the wall, yet she didn't shake. I wanted her to fucking shake. I wanted her to fear me. To hate me. Maybe then she would leave me alone.

I needed her to be the one.

Her obsession was becoming mine.

Her lunacy was becoming contagious.

She was so fucking dark, but my eyes were getting used to the darkness.

With the overpowering need to regain some semblance of power, I unzipped my pants. She broke her stare to look at my cock, with the first real signs of loss of control present as I pulled it out.

I jacked off and made her watch. I wanted her to see that I didn't need her. She would have to watch me get off without her help.

I liked it. I liked seeing the crazed lust surface in the depths of the dark eyes that stared helplessly up at me. I was a sick bastard. I knew this.

I was about to use and abuse her like discarded trash.

It was the only way to break the spell.

Feeling all the fury of my life bubble inside. Feeling all my hate. Feeling all the dark fucking evil that consumed all of who I was, I allowed the cum to leave my body in a rush as I growled. My seed splashed down on her exposed body, covering her in my completion. The cum shot out as I felt all my built up angst flow out with it. Hate exited me and rained down upon her. Hurt exploded from deep inside of my gut and showered against her creamy-white flesh, tainting her purity with my selfish and solo release.

Yet, she was beautiful. So insanely beautiful. The wetness coated her flesh, dripped from her hard nipples, and dampened the angles of her collarbone. My cock remained hard, but I maintained my control. I towered over her cum-covered body with my intent completed. My goal was to humiliate her, shame her, splashing the reality onto her soul, shocking her with the darkness of her situation, I watched as her eyes overflowed with tears, and she finally cried. My crazy stalker finally gave me what I needed. She showed me that she was indeed vulnerable. She was indeed alive.

She finally saw me for the man I was.

"Leave. Leave now."

The big droplets of her misery cascaded down her face as the last of my cum dripped out of me onto her naked body.

I had finally won a battle.

She had seen I was not going to play some sweet high school game with her. She wanted a seat at the adults' table... well, she better be prepared to face what that all means.

"I don't want to see you again. Clean yourself up, and then show yourself out," I said as I put my cock away and went into my bedroom, slamming the door hard.

I knew it wouldn't be as easy as that getting her out of my home... out of my life. When she banged on my bedroom door as she exited the bathroom, I had expected it. But I also needed the door between us so that I could regain some sort of control. I was losing my damn mind touching her, kissing her, seeing her naked...

She was making me as mental as she.

Fuck, I was more mental and needed even more help than she did. What the hell was I thinking fucking a student? I knew better. I wasn't that guy. I wasn't some creeper who needed to get any pussy I could get any chance I had. I didn't need this. It was messy, and I sure as hell didn't do messy.

"D..."

She needed to stop calling me that.

I was her principal. I was her principal!

"I'm sorry. I know how you must be feeling, and I know I messed up by not being honest with you." Her voice was so soft, so vulnerable, so much so that a part of me wanted to open the door, hug her, and tell her everything was going to be all right.

But everything was *not* going to be all right. Never again.

"I tried really hard not to lie to you," she said.

I opened the door wide, feeling crazed. "You tried *hard* not to lie? How can you stand here and say that? You made me believe you had a stalker. You made me think that Kevin was the culprit. You had me get the police involved!"

She shook her head slowly. "No," her voice was so low it sounded close to a whisper, "you did that. I didn't want you to call the police. I also told you that Kevin didn't do anything wrong."

If there was ever a chance of me having an aneurysm in my lifetime, it would have happened right then and there. "Are you going to stand there and act like you did nothing wrong?"

She looked down at the ground, then back up at me. "I won't apologize for forcing our cards. Was it wrong? Yes. Did I deceive you? Yes. But the end result is you and I found each other, and you can't deny that those feelings are there."

"Those feelings were built on the delusions of a mentally unstable woman."

"I'm as stable as you and as stable as anyone else. There's a fine line between lunacy and love. I admit that I balance on it."

"You stalked me, Corrine. Can't you see how crazy that is?"

She shook her head. "I saw what I wanted, and I made it happen. You may not like how I did it—and I apologize for that—but the end result was we got a chance to experience being together when circumstances of life may never have allowed it."

Jesus... she was starting to make sense.

I actually was listening to the madness.

Her voice intoxicated me.

Her beauty lulled me in.

No. No. No.

"What exactly is your planned endgame?" I asked. "Do you really believe we can be together after this?"

"Why not?"

I laughed maniacally. "Why are you acting like this is all normal? You hunted me and I fell in your trap. But I sure as hell won't remain in your cage."

"I'm not going to let you make it sound like you and I weren't forming a connection. I didn't misread that."

"Of course you didn't. There was something," I admitted, hating that I could be adding fuel to her inferno of delusion. "Which is why I'm so fucking pissed. I was a fool. I risked everything for... a ruse." I took a deep breath feeling like the hallway we stood in narrowed with every inhale and exhale. "I'm lucky your mother is not trying to have me fired. She should. She should demand my resignation."

Corrine took a cautious step closer and placed her hand on my chest. "I'm asking for your forgiveness. I apologize for not being the one to tell you. I can only imagine what it felt like."

"Get out now," I demanded. I needed clarity, and this girl was nothing but murky water. "Now, Corrine, or so help me God, I will pick you up and throw you out."

18

CORRINE

Day Two:

He needs time.

I'll be patient.

I'll wait.

But I will watch him closely as he changes his mind.

19

CORRINE

Day Three:

He will love me.

He just doesn't know it yet.

20

CORRINE

Day Four:

I haven't been back to school. He thinks I've left for L.A... maybe I should.

Maybe I... no... he misses me.

I can tell.

21

Corrine

Day Five:

I'm alone.

I'm scared.

I fucked up.

Will he ever forgive me?

22

CORRINE

That Shelly chick better not show up tonight. I would cut a bitch... okay, not really, but I may slash her tires or something.

Does he miss me?

23

CORRINE

"You need to stop camping outside my house, Corrine," Mr. D said as he surprised me by approaching my car window from behind.

I had jumped and nearly screamed because I had no idea that he knew I'd been outside, watching, waiting. I wasn't going to just give up.

"You haven't been to school all week," he said. "I thought you were going to go back to L.A."

I shook my head. "It's even more of a mess in L.A. than it is here. At least here, I have you."

"You don't have me," he said, though his voice wasn't nearly as angry as it had been a few days ago. Was he forgiving me? "You never did. There was no you and me."

"You know that's a lie," I said, confident that what I desired was not that far off from what he wanted. "You said it yourself. You said I was easy to talk to. That I was fun to be around. You said I deserved love."

"You do deserve love," he said.

"Then why are you turning me away?"

"You know why."

"Do you really think I'm some crazy stalker?" I asked.

He laughed. "Are you not? Where have you been for the past week? Oh I know... here. Stalking."

I shrugged. "Okay... maybe I am. But I'm not dangerous or truly psycho." I studied how he just casually stood by my car. It was true. All anger had left him. "You aren't afraid of me, are you?"

He sighed. "I'm afraid *for you*. I don't think you made your decisions with the right mind. I think you had an infatuation with me that maybe wasn't healthy and without knowing this, I took advantage of your weakness." He put his hand on my car door and leaned in. "This was wrong."

"You keep saying that."

"Because it's true."

"No, you say it because it's easier to think that rather than to really dig deep into your feelings."

He smirked. "So now you're giving me shrink talk."

I smiled. "I'm the expert on that." I looked toward his condo. "Can we go inside and talk?"

He was quiet for several moments which I took as a hopeful sign.

He shook his head. "No, I don't think that's a good idea. I don't trust myself."

Even though he was rejecting my idea, my heart skipped a beat that he actually didn't trust his actions. He wanted me. He couldn't deny that fact. And that wasn't just my crazy talking.

"Are you hungry?" I asked. "I know this great Mexican restaurant that some sexy man brought me to once."

He shook his head, ran his hands through his hair, closed his eyes, then looked up at the sky.

I waited in silence.

He reminded me of a knight, slaying the dragons of his mind. I just hoped that the outcome would be... me.

I needed him to choose me.

Finally, after several minutes, he gave a weak smile and nodded. "I'll drive."

Mr. D

I turned off the highway and followed a side road which was the long way to get there. Corrine was fast asleep. I knew she hadn't been sleeping. The dark circles were obvious, but I also knew she had been practically camping outside my place. I should have stopped the stalker game the minute she started, but the vindictive side of me wanted her to suffer a bit. A punishment for her lies. Plus, I'd needed the week to calm down, to think, and to come up with what I wanted.

At my suggestion, she curled up under my jacket and quickly floated off to sleep. It seemed like all she needed was to be in my presence to relax. Rest was something we both needed desperately, but not nearly as much as we needed each other in order to get it. I hadn't been sleeping either. I'd get up in the middle of the night and see her car in the shadows. Knowing she was just steps away, and that I could make all the lonely feelings and pain go away if I would just walk out there and forgive her. If I could just take her in my arms and tell her that I was ready to move past everything and focus on the future.

But was I?

Could I?

After a much longer drive than planned so she could at least get a cat nap, we finally reached the restaurant that sat on an alpine mountain lake.

I couldn't help but smile at Corrine as I pondered how to wake her. I was done with vindictive. I was over being mean. I didn't want to hurt her. I wanted to be the man I was and keep the promises I gave her.

For a week I had tried to make reason out of a fucked up situation. But the only thing I could think of was that Corrine was a lonely woman who had never felt loved. She had never been taught how to get it in a healthy way.

Was she the one to blame? Truly?

Her heart was in the right place even though her mind may have not been.

Very softly, I whispered her name and kissed her warm cheek. She began to stir, a moan mixing with a soft sigh. I brushed my lips against hers, feeling the loving beginnings of a smile. I pulled back enough to watch her eyes gradually flutter awake. The smile disappeared for a short moment but returned when she looked up into my eyes. It had been what felt like an eternity since I saw it, felt it, but I could see the connection was still there. There was an overpowering bond that somehow was still holding us together when every ounce of sanity in my body screamed for me to run.

"Are we there yet?" she asked huskily, while rubbing her eyes.

"We are." I pointed at the beginning of a sunset, dipping beneath the sparkling water of the lake. "The sun's about to set."

Corrine's smile widened, and her eyes brightened as she sat up all the way to take in the scenery. The horizon illuminated a gold that seemed magical against the tranquil water.

I freed her seat belt and then walked over to her side of the car and opened the door. "Let's watch the sunset before we go inside," I suggested as I enclosed her under my arm, snuggling her close, leaning on the hood of my car.

Corrine nuzzled her head against my chest with a soft sigh.

I should still be angry, but I wasn't.

I should stop this before I got her hopes up that there would be something between us in the future.

I should spare her feelings.

Hell... I should spare my own.

But I missed her. I fucking missed the shit out of her, and I didn't care that reason was chanting within my brain. My heart wanted her. My entire being craved to let anything negative go and just accept her for her.

She lifted her face as though she read my mind. As though she could feel how badly I wanted to kiss her. Her lips parted, inviting my mouth, beckoning my touch.

I swear she had the ability of a powerful witch. She could enchant me with just the air she breathed.

She positioned her body closer, pressing tight against my wavering strength. I caved in fully and gave her a passionate kiss, a kiss like the very first night. A kiss that reminded me of why... why I couldn't just turn her away.

It wasn't as simple as saying no. It wasn't easy.

In fact, everything about this situation was a mess. Pure destruction and chaos, but I didn't care. I welcomed it.

I tightened my hold, pulling her in my arms to keep her from slipping away. Everything felt whole again, strong again, but I also didn't trust anything I was feeling.

Maybe I needed to be committed right along with her.

I was a grown-ass man and had no one to blame for my careless decisions but myself...

And I was choosing Corrine.

Reason be damned.

We stood there in silence until the entire sky changed from a copper flame to a dark ember. We held each other, occasionally kissing, stroking, and luxuriating in not being alone. Not fighting what we felt was right even though the universe hollered just how wrong it was.

So wrong.

So twisted.

So unhealthy.

But we both didn't give a fuck.

Get the straitjackets out, because I was going all in.

When we finally entered the restaurant, we were seated at a table with an expansive view of the lake. The lights of the surrounding houses sparkled against the midnight sheen of the water, which was illuminated by the early moonlight. The other diners were lost in their own conversations, giving us the feeling as though we were dining alone. And alone together is exactly what we needed. No judgment, no voices of reason, no harsh comments —just us figuring it out.

Corrine took in the scenery while fiddling with her napkin. I could see she was nervous and didn't know how to hide that blatant fact from me.

I had questions. I knew this dinner wouldn't be easy, and I'm sure she felt the same way. I needed to know that what I was feeling—what I could no longer deny—wasn't just an illusion.

"You seem awfully quiet," I started after the waiter had poured our wine, leaving the bottle behind.

I appreciated that he didn't card Corrine and make her feel uncomfortable. She looked of age, and I most certainly did, so the waiter wasn't doing anything out of the ordinary. I also appreciated that we didn't have to be reminded of her age once again.

She took a sip of the wine that left a trail of red, fingering down the crystal. I watched how she held the glass. Experienced. This was a woman who no doubt had sampled wine far more expensive and coveted than I could ever dream of. And as she drank, all I could think of was that I wanted to hear all the stories of her past. I wanted to know more and take the time to learn all about this girl who was anything but boring.

"So do you," she said.

"Trying to process everything." I reclined back in my chair and rubbed my thumb against the rim of the wine glass. "There's a war going on inside of me."

Corrine looked off toward the illumination on the water, trying to fight back the tears threatening to escape her eyes. "I'm scared I messed up a good thing forever. I wish I hadn't... but... I can't control my thoughts and actions sometimes." She glanced at me with wet eyes. "I know I have issues, but it kills me to know you now think I'm crazy."

"I think we both are a little mad," I said with a small grin to try to lighten the mood. "I don't appreciate being lied to. I don't appreciate starting this relationship on false pretenses, but I have to agree with you... this relationship would never have happened had you not."

"Are you still angry with me?"

"No. I feel we have some things to discuss, a lot to work out, and we have to figure out what our path will be next. But no, I'm not mad."

A smile washed over her breathtakingly beautiful face. "So, does that mean you are considering there being an *us*?"

I took a ragged breath to attempt to steady my composure. The time had come to ask the question haunting me since finding out the truth. I tried to poise myself by taking another drink of my wine. "I need honesty."

She nodded. "I'll give it to you."

"Do you feel you still have an obsession over the teacher in L.A.? It must have been bad if it landed you in the hospital," I asked, keeping my gaze locked on her.

"It was bad," she almost whispered. "But I worked through it. At least with my sickness over him I did. And if you would have kept rejecting me, I can't say it wouldn't have gone really bad with you too. I would like to say I'd be strong enough to fight off the really dark demons, but I don't know."

"How bad was it?" I leaned toward her, reaching for her hand.

"I hate talking about this, but..." The blush on her face began to take over. "He didn't have feelings for me. Never did. It was one-sided completely, but I kept thinking I could make him love me, but when that didn't happen, I got angry. I keyed his car, I spray painted his house, I broke windows... and I set his place on fire." Corrine pulled her hand away and reached for her wine, taking a large swig.

"Jesus..."

She took another deep breath. "He said he wouldn't press charges if I agreed to get help. So, I went away and missed most of my senior year which is why I had to repeat it. But there was no way I could return to the same school because enough people knew and were talking. And there was also the fact he had a restraining order on me. So, I decided to attend Black Mountain Academy." She paused, shrugged, and took another sip of wine. "I guess people would assume I didn't get enough help because I fell hard for another man who was older than me and in a place of authority. I developed a crush for my principal. A sick crush, people would say. I'm sure my shrink would call it Daddy issues, but I can't help who I find attractive. And when I saw you... I thought you were the most gorgeous man I had ever seen. I had to get your attention somehow, and yes, I lied. But I really couldn't think of any other way. The difference with you versus the teacher in L.A. is that you actually seemed to care about me. You saw a side of me that no one saw. You made me feel... loved."

"I fell hard for you too. Otherwise, this wouldn't be nearly as hard. It would have been easy to turn my back on you." She was owed my full honesty as well.

"Really? You fell for me? Do you think there"—she looked around self-consciously, blushing even further—"is a chance that you and I could really be together. Not just in hiding?"

"Well," I said after a long moment's silence. "I think you need to graduate. Which isn't a long time from now." I narrowed my eyes as I took a sip of wine. "As long as you stop missing school, that is. I'll excuse the last week, but no more freebies. No special treatment."

A glow of embarrassment and unease blended together and washed over her cheeks. "Yes. I promise." Corrine allowed her gaze to move from me, to the calm surface of the lake.

"And I'm not saying it's going to be easy, because it's not. We are in different stages of our lives. I don't know what that means. You still have to figure out what you want out of life and I can't be the one holding you back."

She kept her eyes fixed on the moonlight's glow. She remained silent and didn't say anything.

I spoke again, impatient for a response. "Look at me. Talk to me."

She fidgeted beneath my hot glare. "You have to figure out what you want too. Is it me?"

I nodded. "It is." I poured each of us some more wine. "We need to figure out how to make that work, but I'm committed to try if you are."

"It's all I've ever wanted," she said softly, then paused as our waiter approached and placed our entrees before us.

I reached for Corrine's hand and squeezed. My eyes connected with hers, silently letting her know we were going to be fine. The waiter was rapid and in moments, gone.

"Are you okay with keeping our relationship a secret?" I asked, my voice low. "I have to still remain Mr. D to you for much of the day. You will still be a student at Black Mountain Academy, and that situation could start to take its toll."

Corrine nodded as she took a bite of her enchilada. "I am. We don't have a choice. But I get nervous that you'll want someone older like that Shelly woman." She stiffened in her chair and reached for her wine with a shaky hand. "I don't want to eventually be seen as just a kid to you."

"If I saw you as just a kid, I wouldn't even be sitting here with you." My voice was deep and hoarse, my throat tight as if reluctant to let the words escape. I stopped eating, blew out a breath and said, "I know you had it rough in the past. I know you have never truly had someone love and stand by your side. I also know you are going to struggle believing that I would. But you need to believe me when I say this. No matter what you fear, I'd never cheat on you. I'd never disrespect you like that. I broke it off with Shelly the minute you and I had sex."

Corrine took a long drink of her wine. "I'm going to start seeing someone... a therapist. I know what I did was wrong. And I also really want you and me to work." She looked down at her plate and then giggled. "And I really don't want to burn down your house after our first fight."

I shook my head and nearly choked on my food as I burst out in laughter. "I think that's a good idea. Arson isn't really on my list of things I want to deal with." I looked up into her eyes, growing serious. "I plan to be by your side while you battle the monsters. I told you I'd help slay the dragons. You aren't in this alone."

She softly touched my hand. Her palm was warm, smooth, and delivered chills racing up and down my spine. She looked deep within my eyes, and I wondered how I could ever resist a woman like her? She was in my blood.

She may have forced her way in but was there regardless.

"I've never felt that way in my life. Never," she said.

"Well then we're even. Because you sure as hell have introduced me to a wave of intense feelings myself. It's like a rollercoaster. Thrilling."

She winked. "I like hearing I got your blood pumping."

I chuckled. "Yeah, you definitely woke up something I had pushed deep inside. I'll give you that." With a mischievous smile, I asked, "Do you want to get out of here? Let's go home."

She glanced at her plate and then mine. "We haven't finished eating yet."

"All I want right now is to pick you up, toss you over my shoulder, and carry you out of this restaurant. I want you alone so I can show you just how much you have gotten into my head, my heart, and my body." I pushed my chair back, grabbed my wallet, and placed a pile of cash on the table.

"We didn't get the bill yet—"

"Corrine..." I reached out my hand and stared down into her eyes.

She took a moment to think about it, playfully acting as if she were actually considering just keeping her seat. Finally, with a sly smile, she stood up and took my hand.

"Let's go home, Mr. D."

24

MR. D

I'd wanted Corrine back in my bed for days now, and my desire had only grown even more as we spoke so openly over dinner. It took everything I had not to sweep her into my arms on the side of the road and have my way with her before we reached my place. But I wasn't going to rush it and not give her the sensual and seductive, that we both needed, to set the balance right again. Our last sexual experience had been a hate fuck, and I wanted to correct the wrong. Tonight, I didn't want to just have sex with her. I wanted to make love to her.

Once we reached the bedroom, I let go of Corrine's hand to light a candle on the nightstand. It gave just enough light to cast us in a soft, romantic glow. When I turned to face her again, my heart skipped a beat. Corrine was pure perfection sprawled out naked on the bed. The time away from me left her hungry, wanting, and ready. We were on the same page in that regard. Wide, sultry eyes watched me undress before her.

I towered over her, placing my palms on the mattress. "I love when you look at me that way."

Corrine arched her body, attempting to make contact with my chest. "And how am I looking at you?" she questioned, gazing even deeper into my eyes.

"Like you belong to me." I lowered my face to hers, nipping at her lips. "You're mine, Corrine. Others may not know it yet, but it's only a matter of time. Mine," I murmured against her mouth.

My gaze locked on hers before I flipped her over on her stomach. My hands rested on her hips as I compressed the full weight of my chest against her back. I pressed my lips to her ear and whispered, "I like seeing the firmness of this bare ass... waiting for me."

Corrine moaned softly and lifted her bottom to press against the hardness of my cock. "I love feeling you pressed against me." Her voice was almost a purr.

"You were so beautiful at dinner being honest and more real than any woman I've ever met," I whispered while one hand traveled to the silky smoothness of her sex. My fingertip pressed past the folds and dipped into her warmth.

Corrine cried out as my finger gently prodded in and out of her wetness.

"I don't want you to leave this bed again," I growled into her ear. Her wetness intensified as she ground against my hand, urging me on.

"I'm here as long as you'll have me," she moaned, her muscles tensing as she neared the edge. "Yes... I want to be yours. Only yours."

"Come for me. I want to feel you come against my hand."

That was all it took. I held her body tight against mine as she climaxed, absorbing the passionate spasms of her release.

With one fluid motion, I rolled her over and drove my hardness deep within. Corrine's head flew back as she cried out. Her fingers clutched desperately at my back. The sound of her pleasured cry triggered a desire to hear her moans over and over again. I could think of nothing else but rocking into her until her cries became a scream of ecstasy.

Corrine wrapped her legs around my back, pulling me deeper within. "D..." she gasped before bringing her lips to mine.

I thrust my tongue past her lips as I drove in and out of her heat. I closed my eyes, soaking in the sensation of wave after wave of pleasure that washed over me. I groaned against her lips as my climax began to escalate.

I eased back and thrust into her again, drawing the desired scream to escape past our kiss. She arched against me, tilting her hips up as I pressed deeper and harder.

When Corrine screamed out my name, her muscles pulsating around my cock, it was all I needed to pump my release deep within her.

I allowed the sounds of her passion to push me over the edge. I allowed the sensations of satisfaction, strength, and love, to wash over me.

We slept, we caressed, we kissed, we made love again, and then we slept once more. It was a broken record repeating, and I never planned to fix it.

When I woke up, I saw the glass slider open and Corrine standing naked, overlooking the fountain outside.

My lower body seized with a deep longing to have her again. Corrine's long hair blanketed down her naked back, almost reaching her luscious backside. The delicate curve of her bottom made me hungry for more.

I wanted her now.

I walked to the balcony to join her. Taking a quick moment to adjust to the chill of the morning air, I moved to where she stood.

Wrapping my arms around her body, I murmured against her cool neck, "I woke up and you were gone. Don't leave me again."

She turned her head to look over her shoulder, her eyes twinkling with mischief. "And if I do?" she teased as she pressed her bottom to my hardness.

I slid my hands around her waist and pulled her tighter against me. She didn't resist, but instead, positioned her body so that her ass rested against my lengthening desire.

"I would have to punish you," I said with a nip to her ear. "And I would love every second of it."

Corrine released a soft moan, tilting her head back in sweet surrender. She pressed her ass even closer, allowing the tip of my erection to enter past her tiny back hole. Not all the way, but enough to feel the tight heat of her taboo channel. I splayed my hands across her bare mound and toyed with her clit, swirling my fingertip in circles the way I knew she loved. I was beginning to understand every inch of Corrine's body and had mastered the skill of causing her body to hum.

I was a good student, determined to study hard.

"Then I'll just have to accept my punishment like a good girl," she replied, sighing contentedly.

With the tip of my penis still teasing her entrance, I growled, "Maybe taking you here is exactly the punishment you deserve."

I twirled her to face me, my hands hugging the roundness of her behind. Inhaling deeply, intoxicated by her scent, I moaned.

I slipped a finger under her chin and tipped her face up to me. My lips met hers. They were smooth and soft, cool from her morning outing to the deck.

I couldn't help pressing forward, driving my ready cock against her heat.

The kiss was much like the ones we had shared, yet there was something different about it. There was a new hunger, a new want. When my arms slipped around her waist, my finger sliding into the crevice of her behind, there was no tension or tightening from her. Every inch closer my finger got to her puckered hole, her body seemed to soften against mine. With a hungry press of my fingertip into her tightness, her full submission was obvious. This vixen hungered for this, and I needed to make sure she never hungered again.

As I guided her back inside the room so we could explore a new step in our relationship, the doorbell rang.

We both froze. It was early in the morning, so an unexpected guest seemed even more unlikely at this hour.

"Someone's at the door," Corrine whispered, her voice laced in panic.

"Ignore it," I said, feeling my stomach drop.

I had no idea who it could be. I glanced at the clock on the bedside table and saw it wasn't quite 6:00 a.m. yet. There was no way it could be Shelly even if she hadn't taken my calling it off seriously. It was too early.

The doorbell rang again, followed by a pounding on the door.

I reached for my sweats quickly and pulled them on. I then reached for my shirt as I really didn't feel like opening the door bare-chested. Corrine had reached for her own shirt and sweats and was getting dressed as quickly as she could.

"Just stay here," I said. "I'll go check it out."

When I approached the door and looked out the peephole, I didn't recognize the woman on the other side. It wasn't someone I knew. It didn't appear to be law enforcement or anything in the emergency nature. Wrong place possibly?

I opened the door. "Can I help you?"

"Drew Dawson?" she asked, and the minute she spoke, and I got a good look at her, I knew who she was.

Corrine's mother.

"Ms. Parker. How can I help you?" I had no intentions of inviting her in, so whatever she had to say to me would have to be done on my doorstep.

"I'm assuming my daughter's here," she said.

Fuck.

"How did you find out where I live?" I needed to stall to figure out how to handle this situation. I could lie, but she wouldn't be here if she didn't already know the answer to that question.

"I know people in Black Mountain, and when Corrine wasn't at the house when I arrived... well, it wasn't hard." She looked over my shoulder and then back at me. "Are you going to let me inside or shall I call the school board concerned over my daughter's whereabouts?"

Sighing deeply, I opened the door all the way and stepped aside.

She marched in with full confidence and called out, "Corrine, come on. Get your stuff. We're leaving."

Corrine walked out of my bedroom with wide eyes and open mouth. "Mom? What are you doing here?"

"Cleaning up another one of your messes." She pointed at me. "I got a call from Mr. Dawson and was forced to cut my trip short to deal with this." She glanced at Corrine's bare feet. "You have shoes?

Come on, let's get out of here. We have a flight to catch in a couple of hours, and you still need to pack."

"Flight? To where?" Corrine asked. "I can't just leave. I have school." Corrine looked at me with worry washed all over her face. "If I miss any more school, I won't graduate."

"Oh, you'll graduate," Candy snapped. "Mr. Dawson is going to make damn sure of it. Aren't you, Mr. Dawson?"

"She really needs to finish out the year. There isn't much time left—"

"I would hate to get the board involved in this matter," she interrupted.

"Where are we going?" Corrine asked. "I don't want to leave Black Mountain right now."

"You're going back to St. Mary's for a much longer duration this time." She looked me over and then said between clenched teeth. "Clearly the last visit didn't take."

Corrine took a step back in retreat. "I don't need to go back there. I'm fine." She darted her eyes to me and then to her mother. "I know how this looks, but it's different. It's not what you think?"

Candy didn't even look at me but said, "Mr. Dawson, how old are you?"

I didn't answer.

Candy then asked, "And Corrine, how old are you?" When Corrine didn't respond right away, she added, "At least you didn't burn down this man's house. I'm clearly getting off cheap by coming before you do." She then spun on her heels to face me head on. "And you! Are you a fool? I told you over the phone all about Corrine, and yet... here you are. With her!"

"I can assure you that my eyes are wide open to the situation," I said.

Candy huffed and shook her head. "Maybe you should book yourself a room right next to hers."

"Ms. Parker, I know you are a busy woman. And I'm more than happy to help Corrine—"

"Help Corrine? There's no helping her," she interrupted.

She looked back at Corrine. "I don't have time for this. I have another movie shoot coming up. A big one that will have me overseas for quite some time. I can't be worrying about my loony daughter causing issues here in the States. So, get your stuff, and let's get out of here."

"Mom, please. This isn't like L.A. D and I have something more. I'm happy. It may not be normal, but it's not like before."

"Ms. Parker..."

"Mr. Dawson, I'm going to look past the fact that I'm picking my daughter up at your place. I'm going to pretend this entire situation with you and my daughter never occurred. I'm also going to leave you be here in Black Mountain, but I expect you to do the same. Leave Corrine alone, or you'll not like what my next move will be."

"I'm not leaving!" Corrine shouted. "I'm not going back there, and you can't make me. I'm a legal adult, and we aren't doing anything wrong."

Candy's eyes narrowed and her lips pursed together. "You *are* leaving. You may think just because you're nineteen that I have no control. First of all, I control the purse strings, or have you forgotten? Secondly, unless you want to destroy this man's career, you will do what I say. You may not have burned down his house, but if you refuse to go with me, I'll burn down his entire life. I know for a fact the Black Mountain Academy board will not appreciate knowing their principal had sex—multiple times I'm sure—with a mentally unstable student who had just spent time in a psychiatric unit. If that doesn't sound like taking advantage of a situation, I don't know what does." She looked at me and placed her hands on her hips. "Don't push me. I'm not an enemy you want, Mr. Dawson."

In defeat, Corrine grabbed her stuff and exited my house with tears streaming down her face. I didn't say a word. She didn't say a word. Her mother had spoken, and I had yet to figure out how to respond.

25

CORRINE

"I didn't think we'd be seeing you back here, Corrine," Dr. Redmond said as he sat across from me with pen in hand and notebook on his lap.

"I didn't exactly have a choice in the matter," I said, hating that I was once again in this very familiar room about to have my brain dissected again.

"You chose to engage in the same behavior that brought you here in the first place. Correct? That was a choice you made," he said.

"I suppose." I didn't want to say much. All he would do is write it down and use it against me later.

"Tell me about this..." he looked down at this notebook, "Drew Dawson. Your mother tells me that he was the principal at the school you were attending. She also told me that you snuck to that school without her knowing with the intention of stalking him."

"That's not true," I snapped. "She knew I was going to Black Mountain Academy. She just doesn't pay attention to the things I do. And no, I didn't go there with the intentions of stalking him. It just happened... but it's not like you think."

Dr. Redmond continued, "She also said that she has spoken with Mr. Dawson, and he has agreed to not make issue of this situation."

"Make issue?" I asked, not sure what he was saying. And had my mother been in conversation with D after I left?

"What you did is a crime. With your history, Mr. Dawson could have really made problems for you, but your mother got him to agree to forget this unfortunate situation. You should be grateful for that."

Unfortunate situation?

"I may have started to revert to the old me at first," I began. "And I didn't start my relationship with Mr. D with honesty, but something changed as he started to care about me."

"Did you feel that Mr. Harrison cared about you as well?"

"No. I wanted him to. I thought I could convince him to. And when he didn't, I got mad... obviously."

"But Mr. D—is that what you call him? You feel that he genuinely cares about you, in a romantic way?"

I didn't want to tell Dr. Redmond exactly how intense our feelings were for each other, even in such a short time. For one, I didn't think he'd believe me. And second, I didn't want to get D in trouble if Dr. Redmond decided to report him or something.

"It became something different. Yes," I said.

"Then why did he allow you to come here?" the doctor asked. "From what your mother said, he was happy to have you taken from Black Mountain and admitted into St. Mary's."

"That's not true." Although the feeling of wanting to check every door in the hospital began to take over.

Mr. D wouldn't want this.

He wouldn't have allowed me to go with my mother if he had a choice.

Would he have?

"Your mother also said that he is aware of your past."

"Can we stop talking about what my mother said?" I snapped, feeling the urge to storm out of the office. "Ask me if you want the truth. My mother sees things her way and always has. I'm done talking about my mother."

"She comes from a place of concern," he said.

"Concern for herself. Concern for her career. Do you know that the media believes I'm in rehab right now... again? My mother would rather the world believes I'm a cocaine addict than a woman in the search for love." I took a deep, calming breath. "Do I have some issues to work through? Yes. We talked about them the last time I was here. I know I have insecurities, abandonment issues, trust issues, and I struggle with OCD. I know this, and frankly, so does Mr. D. But I also plan to get continued help to cope with those things. But Mr. D said he would be there every step of the way to help me. To be with me."

"And you believe he could be of help? Or do you think it could make things worse? What if he does reject you? What then?"

The doctor's words were like a tsunami of ice-cold water engulfing me. I hated him. I hated this place. No one would understand. No one would get me... other than D.

But where was he?

Why did he let me go?

Was that the end?

"Knowing he's not here," the doctor continued, "does that make you want to lash out? Do you want to burn down his home like you did with Mr. Harrison?"

"No," I said softly.

"What if he doesn't want to be with you? What if he never wanted to be with you?"

God, his words stung.

"It would make me... sad," I admitted.

"Not angry?"

I shook my head in defeat. "Not angry. I would have to accept it and eventually move on. But," I looked into Dr. Raymond's eyes, "I really feel like there is something there. I don't think I was completely delusional in believing so. And the feelings inside of me aren't crazy. It's love. I feel love and not obsession."

Dr. Redmond nodded and smiled.

A voice came from the door behind me. "Good, because I have the same feelings."

I turned in surprise to see D standing in the doorway. He was in a suit, appeared all business, but there was a warm smile on his face and his eyes lit up as they connected with mine.

"Excuse me for interrupting," he said. "I was hoping I could have some time alone to speak with Corrine."

"Corrine? Is that okay with you," Dr. Raymond asked with a raised eyebrow.

I nodded, not sure why I suddenly wanted to burst into tears.

Dr Raymond stood up and said, "I'm going to leave you two alone so you can talk then." He placed his palm on my shoulder. "Keep up the work on yourself, Corrine. You deserve peace, and you most certainly deserve love." He then nodded at D and exited his office.

I sat in the chair, stunned and trying to make sense of what was going on. D was in L.A., at St. Mary's, and standing before me. He had followed me here. Came for me... for me.

"What are you doing here?" I asked as my voice cracked.

He walked over to me and sat in the chair next to mine. "You didn't think I would just let you be taken out of my house and not do anything about it, did you?"

"But my mother..."

"I don't care about your mother," he said with his jaw locking. "And frankly, I don't believe you do as well."

"But she made threats."

He nodded. "She did. But one thing you may not know about me is that I don't scare easy. I don't allow anyone to hold anything over me, blackmail me, or threaten me. If she wants to go to war, then we will. But at the same time, I believe your mother isn't going to care what you do now that she is busy with a movie."

"I agree. As long as I stay out of her hair, she doesn't care what I do. Out of sight, out of mind," I said, hating that I spoke the truth, but it was.

"And we need to get you back to Black Mountain pronto because you have your senior year to finish and a diploma to earn."

My eyes darted around the room, now truly realizing Dr. Redmond wasn't the person calling the shots. "But I'm here. I can't just leave."

"Yes, you can. You signed yourself in, and you can sign yourself out. I also met with Dr. Redmond before you did, and we spoke. He has his concerns, which are valid. But I don't really care what he or anyone thinks at this point. I only care what you feel. What is it that you want?"

"I want you," I said with a smile and a rush of happiness nearly suffocating me.

"And I want you," he said, reaching out for my hand and pulling me up into his arms.

After several moments, I broke away from the embrace, fearful that this was all too good to be true. "So, what does this mean? What happens now?"

"Go get your stuff, sign yourself out as the capable and sane adult that you are, and we head home. We close the door on this chapter and open a new one."

"You don't think I'm crazy?"

"It keeps you interesting," he said with a mischievous grin.

"You don't think I'm obsessive?"

"No more than me, and it's a toss-up as to who is more at this point."

It took me a moment to truly grasp what he was saying. To really listen to the words I was hearing.

He wanted me. He chose me. He fought for me. He didn't want to be without me, and he didn't want to leave me alone.

Leaning down and kissing me softly on the lips, he then said, "It's my turn now."

"Your turn?" I asked, confused.

"To stalk *you*."

.   .   .

The End

Want more of this delicious taste of forbidden?

Be sure to check out.

CAPTIVE BRIDE

You will take this bride.

To have and to hold from this day forward.

Till death do you part.

This will be your solemn vow.

. . .

You have no choice.

Trapped in a twisted and dark courtship with a secret woman who needs my strength to survive, I will be wed.

Walking the thin line between lunacy and reality, I am now the protector of my future captive bride.

So, I have no choice but to recite the vows.

I take thee.

In this arranged matrimony.

Until we are parted by death.

ABOUT THE AUTHOR

Alta Hensley is a USA TODAY bestselling author of hot, dark and dirty romance. She is also an Amazon Top 10 bestselling author. Being a multi-published author in the romance genre, Alta is known for her dark, gritty alpha heroes, sometimes sweet love stories, hot eroticism, and engaging tales of the constant struggle between dominance and submission.

She lives in a log cabin in the woods with her husband, two daughters, and an Australian Shepherd. When she isn't battling the bats, and watching the deer, she is writing about villains who always get their love story and happily ever after.

As a gift for being my reader, I would like to offer you a FREE book.

DELICATE SCARS

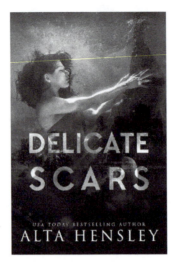

Get your copy now! ~

https://dl.bookfunnel.com/tnpuad5675

I was going to ruin her.

I knew it the moment I laid eyes on her. She was too naive, too innocent.

I would wrap her in the darkness of my world till she no longer craved the light... only me.

I should walk away, leave her clean and untouched... but I won't.

I hold her delicate heart in my scarred fist and I have no intention of letting go.

It all started with a book... doesn't that sound crazy?

For your entire world to come crashing down around you over research for a book?

But that is what it felt like the moment I met him.

My world tilted. Nothing made sense any more.

I only know he became like a drug to me... and I shook with need till my next fix.

Join Alta's Facebook Group for Readers for access to deleted scenes, to chat with me and other fans and also get access to exclusive giveaways:
Alta's Private Facebook Room

Facebook: https://www.
facebook.com/AltaHensleyAuthor/

Amazon: https://www.amazon.com/Alta-Hensley/e/B004G5A6LI

Twitter: https://twitter.com/AltaHensley

Website: www.altahensley.com

Instagram: https://instagram.com/altahensley

Bookbub: https://www.bookbub.com/authors/alta-hensley

TikTok: https://www.tiktok.com/@altahensley

Goodreads: https://www.goodreads.com/author/show/4491649.Alta_Hensley

Join her mailing list: https://readerlinks.com/l/727720/nl

ALSO BY ALTA HENSLEY

Lavish Corruption

Forbidden